Pensione Anastasia

Books by Alice Heard Williams

Poetry

Anna Comes Today!

When Wild Parrots Fly

Hey, Madame Matisse!

Novels

Seeking the High Yellow Note

Remembering Piero

Pensione Anastasia

Pensione Anastasia

Alice Heard Williams

Alice Heard Williams

Copyright © 2006 by Alice Heard Williams.
Library of Congress Control Number: 2006905781
ISBN :   Hardcover   1-4257-2109-5
                     Softcover   1-4257-2108-7

All rights reserved. No part of this book may be reproduced or transmitted in any form or by any means, electronic or mechanical, including photocopying, recording, or by any information storage and retrieval system, without permission in writing from the copyright owner.

This is a work of fiction. Names, characters, places and incidents either are the product of the author's imagination or are used fictitiously, and any resemblances to any actual persons, living or dead, events or locales is entirely coincidental.

This book was printed in the United States of America.

To order additional copies of this book, contact:
Xlibris Corporation
1-888-795-4274
www.Xlibris.com
Orders@Xlibris.com
33435

CONTENTS

INTRODUCTION..9

ONE: A Surprise Encounter at the Temple of Bassae..............................13

TWO: Disaster at the Temple of Zeus; an Accident at Delphi................30

THREE: Death on Constitution Square. Or Is It Murder?.....................52

FOUR: Scotland Yard on the Case 72

FIVE: An Amulet Appears..88

SIX: From Belgravia to Soho to the Earls Court Road 100

SEVEN: Uncle Scopas Pays a Call...111

EIGHT: Phaedra Arrives from Corinth 124

NINE: A Guiness Party at the Man in the Moon Pub
    on Portobello Road 139

TEN: Coffee near the British Museum..154

ELEVEN: Summer Finale in Athens 165

TWELVE: Mozart's Magic Flute at Glyndebourne...............................176

ACKNOWLEDGMENTS 183

READER'S COMMENTS ON *REMEMBERING PIERO*...................185

Dedicated to my readers who embraced Vincent Van Gogh in *Seeking the High Yellow Note* and Piero della Francesca in *Remembering Piero*, readers who have supported me in all of my work with such enthusiasm.

INTRODUCTION

Late 2006 should see the opening of the new archeological museum at the foot of the Acropolis in Athens. The structure will stand as a symbol of the Greek government's belief in the Parthenon as the most important symbol of Greek national identity and thereby of the desire to see all the Parthenon sculptures reunited within it. So how propitious that this year, 2006, sees also the publication of art historian Alice Heard Williams' novel Pensione Anastasia. A narrative of fictional plunder of a Greek artifact but one that resonates with all the factual ramifications of real plunder of a country's past.

The plot revolves around an amulet with a low relief carving of Apollo possibly by Phidias which for centuries since its discovery by a shepherd had been passed on father to son for successive generations and kept hidden near by the Temple of Bassae dedicated to Apollo. The novel is set in the 1970s when the present protector of the amulet, a shepherd with no heirs, decides to give the amulet to the Athens Archeological Museum to become part of public heritage. When the shepherd discovers it to be stolen, his suspicions naturally fall on a group of British students at the Bassae site. His suspicions receive a sympathetic response from the leader of the Study Tour, Professor Maria Crawford. "I understand how you might think a British Group had taken it. After all we took away your treasures from the Parthenon those many years ago."

She offers to contact the police on the distraught shepherd's behalf. From that moment events escalate—a hit and run resulting in the shepherd's death; a botched smuggling of the amulet to England in one of the student's luggage; a series of threats from the radical Greek Cypriot organization, who had stolen it to raise funds for their cause. Police recovery of the amulet and British Museum involvement with regard to its authenticity lead us into the realm of genuine artifacts versus fakes versus acceptable copies. Along with burgeoning love interest between study tour students, between a student and a police inspector involved in the case—all this makes for a riveting read whilst also addressing the serious issues that today are still as pertinent regarding art theft as they were in the past. The plot concludes with the return of the authentic amulet to Greece, to its cultural roots, and the love interests resolved.

On a more personal level, Alice Williams' novel constitutes her creative return, and a thank you to Art Historical Academe by way of this fictional gem.

Annela Twitchin, art historian and writer
London, March, 2006

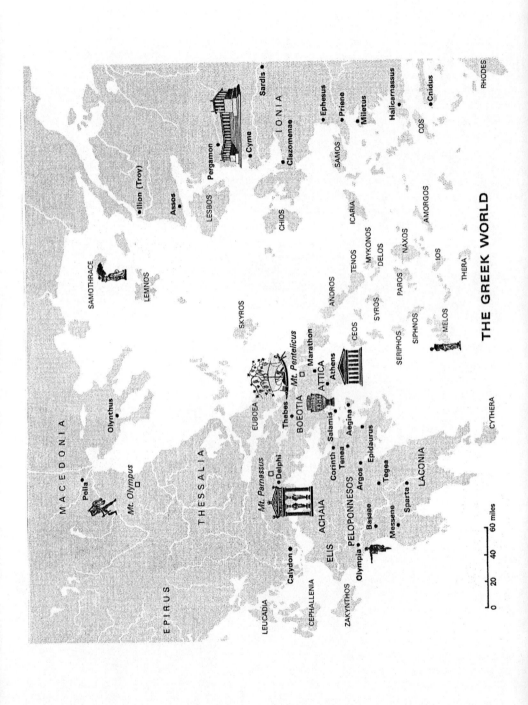

ONE

A Surprise Encounter at the Temple of Bassae

Breakfasts at the Pensione Anastasia are simple, only coarse bread, jam and fruit, but the aromatic fragrance of the coffee brings members of the group downstairs promptly chattering like mockingbirds. Most of them are shy and reserved, properly so for English university students Emma Darling thinks, not vocal Americans. But then, Greek inns are noisy in any case she reflects, hurrying downstairs, heels tapping. All that marble underfoot, marble on the walls, creating reverberating waves of sound. Spotting a table beside a window, she sinks into the soft chair and unfolds a snowy napkin; "serviette" her English friends would say. Emma waits for her roommate Jane.

In spite of tiny cubicles for bedchambers and somewhat rustic plumbing, the Anastasia is both ancient and pleasant, set up against the village street, with vineyards and the ever-present olive trees of Greece for a backdrop. The carefully tended young grape vines marching across terraces behind the building already bear tiny, hard pellets of fruit. In appearance the pensione does not resemble the usual whitewashed squares and rectangles of village buildings, rather the walls are a mellowed, honeyed ocher punctuated by arched doorways and windows. Even landlocked Olympia pays tribute here to Renaissance Italy, Emma thinks, wondering about the origin of the old inn.

Her student group has spent several days studying in depth the temples on the Acropolis, from the glorious Parthenon to the small, exquisite ruins of the Temple of Athena Nike. They explored the Byronic associations of the ruins of the Temple of Poseidon at Sounion by the sea, the theater at Epidarus, the Temple of Apollo, Corinth. Now remain only the Temple of Zeus at Olympia, the Temple of Apollo at Bassae, the complex ruins at Delphi and a return visit on their final day to Athens, where they will study sculpture in the two major Athens museums.

The town of Olympia, their base, is little more than a village, but its ruins of the Temple of Zeus are the premier surviving remnants of the archaic age of Greek temple structure. The Pensione Anastasia provides both cheap accommodation and a charming locus to experience village life for the London University students, traveling with their professor of Greek Art. *And today we go to Bassae!* Emma smiles in anticipation.

She looks out on a street covered with layers of dust shimmering like gossamer in the pearly morning light. A few housewives, dressed in funereal black, frowns on their faces, plod toward the market. Two goat boys herd half a dozen nimble kids, necks ringed with tiny, tinkling bells, prancing their way toward upland pastures. Old men of the village shuffle toward the *taverna* where they will idle away the morning in a haze of tobacco smoke hovering overhead, talking, dozing, gossiping, sipping powerful black coffee from tiny cups. One can hardly believe it is 1974 in this part of the world.

Emma spreads a bit of jam on a crust of the hard bread. The jam is very good, thick, studded with pieces of apricot, rich and delicious. How strange to be here, far away from London and the dreary spring rains of April. Her room in Richard and Frances Belfrage's flat on Chesham Place, tucked away from the humming bustle of Knightsbridge and Belgravia in central London, seems remote. As for Crozet, that village hidden in the layered folds of the Blue Ridge mountains near Charlottesville, Virginia, her home, why Crozet is a planet away.

Emma sighs, thoughts on her mother and father, lecturers at the University of Virginia in Charlottesville, her two younger brothers Adam and Joe. How she misses them! She wills herself to push away all thoughts of Virginia, to think instead of a year of study at London University coming to a close before returning to America to find a job. She has a comfortable place to stay with friends of her parents, the Belfrages, in their Belgravia flat. And now, on this tour, an opportunity to study the sculpture and architecture of Greece first hand, led by the eccentric, exasperating but brilliant art historian, Maria Crawford. Her spirits lift and she forgets to feel homesick. She takes another sip of the fragrant coffee. Greece is wonderful, with the air smelling of rosemary and wild thyme.

"Excuse me, Miss. Coffee?" The young waitress interrupts her thoughts, offering pitchers of hot milk and coffee. Emma nods.

As the girl effortlessly pours the dual streams into her cup, she notices the simple but clean white blouse with drawstring tie at the neck, the faded blue skirt. She wears cheap thong sandals. Her hair is curly, dark like a martin's wing. Eyes under well-shaped black brows shine like clear, dark pools. She is attractive, but unsmiling.

"You come from England?" she asks, looking intently at Emma.

"I'm living in London for a year to study art history, but I'm an American."

The girl's face brightens. "I have cousins there. In Houston. My cousin is a cook on a freighter. He and his wife live in Houston," she finishes proudly. Emma smiles at the girl's pronunciation. "Hoos-ton". Just the way her British friends say it.

"Your English is very good. Do you study it in school?"

"Not there." Her reply is scornful. "My brother Michael is a travel agent in London. He taught me. He has been working there for five years." Unmistakable pride in her voice.

"What is your name?"

"Lydia," she replies, squaring thin shoulders. Emma guesses she is about fifteen.

"A very pretty name, Lydia. My name is Emma, Emma Darling. What will you do when your schooling is finished, Lydia?"

"Work here full time, at the Anastasia, until my younger brothers finish school. Then I'll go to England. My brother has promised he can find a job for me." Solemnly she regards Emma.

Emma's room-mate Jane appears, quickly slips into the chair, murmuring her apology. Some problem getting enough water for the bath, it seems. Emma smiles. Jane has a difficult time adjusting to foreign plumbing and strange food.

"Before you ask Jane, this is a good breakfast, even though it is simple. Coffee, jam and bread. The jam is apricot and delicious. The coffee is heavenly."

"Well, a cup of tea would be nice," Jane answers wistfully.

"Don't even think about it. Not with this marvelous coffee!" Emma grins.

She admires Jane Hale, who seems unsure of herself in so many ways. She is mildly dyslexic, and completing the written papers for Maria Crawford makes Jane suffer. The dictionary simply grows out of her hands as she works, she tells Emma. But her insight into art, particularly sculpture, is remarkable, her opinions succinct and original. But she is shy about expressing her thoughts.

Some students in the group respond like parrots, choosing their pronouncements from the quotes of well-known writers on Greek art. However, the parrots must be careful about showing off their pilfered statements in the presence of Miss Crawford, who does not suffer fools gladly and is capable, even enjoys, cutting the offender to ribbons in front of the assembled group, if she detects sloppy, regurgitated responses.

Jane's level brows and brown hair kept in place by a narrow black headband compliment grey eyes filled with tiny flecks of green. Tall and thin, clothes well-cut, she cares nothing for fashion and is indifferent to her appearance, wearing little makeup, totally absorbed in her studies.

When Jane shyly asked Emma to room with her on the trip, Emma jumped at the chance. They get on amazingly well, Emma from a household of rowdy, loving younger brothers and adoring parents, Jane, the only child of divorce who lives with her mother in a house on Montpelier Square, not far from the Belfrage flat.

Jane, sent off to a boarding school in the English Midlands when she was eight, learned to wash in cold water and run a mile before breakfast each morning. She hated school until a discerning teacher identified Jane's problem. Dyslexia, not stupidity was responsible for her deplorable spelling and her somewhat hesitant speech. Things improved markedly from that point, but the shyness and quiet nature remain.

Back home they would call it low self-esteem, Emma muses as she watches Jane carefully butter a section of bread. But I don't care for blatant self-esteem, and Jane is so restful to be around. And very pretty. The realization comes to her as she covertly watches Jane over the rim of her cup.

They linger over coffee, talking of the day's plan to visit to the Temple of Apollo at Bassae. It is almost time to climb on to the coach when they leave the dining room and hurry upstairs to fetch notebooks. The room has already been tidied by someone, pillows fluffed and the simple blue crinkle bedspreads smoothed over the beds.

As Emma reaches for her notebook on the bureau she notices her top drawer is open about two inches.

Did I leave it that way? she asks herself, frowning. She opens the drawer and finds her passport in place, a letter from her mother beneath. But hadn't the letter been on top of the passport? Emma peers into the small mirror over the chest. Solemn blue eyes in a pretty, intelligent face framed by sandy, waving hair regard her. She is sure the letter had been on top! Who could have moved it? Looked at her passport? Jane? Surely not! Jane's guileless nature is incompatible with anything underhand like snooping. Someone at Pensione Anastasia? But why? The blue eyes widen as she gazes out the window. Why?

"You didn't open my drawer did you, Jane?"

"No, I did not. What's wrong?" Jane looks at Emma. "Is anything missing?"

"Not really," Emma replies. "It's just that I put a letter from home on top of my passport when I read it over last night before going to sleep. Now, the passport is on top, the letter on the bottom."

Jane's wide grey eyes open wider. "Could someone have messed about while we were at breakfast? They could have done, you know, when they made the beds."

A hurried tap on the door and a shout, "Coach is revving up!" from one of the students sends them flying, thoughts of the great temple at Bassae filling their minds, the incident of the riffled drawer forgotten.

~

Columns of the Temple of Apollo at Bassae stand high, roofless on a remote hilltop, surrounded by wildflowers and grasses, strong winds mournfully whistling and whirling around the site. Built around 400 BC, it is a Doric temple, said to have been designed by Ictinus, the architect of the Parthenon. But because of its remote position, hidden in the mountains of Arcadia, it was lost to the western world until rediscovered by explorers in 1765.

Provincial in both position and workmanship, it nonetheless incorporated dramatic new features: a side door to the *cella*, or main room, with the cult statue of Apollo facing the door. Ionic capitals of unusual design with high, swinging volutes rest on engaged columns along each side. For the first time, a single column in front of the back wall is of a new type, the Corinthian order, small volutes at each corner with acanthus leaves girdling the column beneath.

The Corinthian style provides more versatility than the Ionic capital, for it offers the same aspect from all sides. Emma looks over her notes on the details of the Bassae ruins as the bus chugs along.

She has done her homework on this type of column. It became popular much later, and mainly in Rome. The addition of the acanthus leaves at Bassae marks a new range of floral decoration, widely applied to various elements of Greek architecture as it gained acceptance.

Another innovation of Bassae was an interior frieze, running around the top of the wall inside the *cella*; its subject, the battle of the Greeks and the Amazons. Emma feels a mounting excitement at the thought of studying the actual ruins of the remote temple she has pored over so carefully in her books.

The coach winds its way upward; the scenery becomes wilder. Only an occasional village dots the roadside and fewer hillsides are planted with olives. The countryside takes on a more primitive, untamed aspect.

What a poor land Greece is, Emma thinks, looking out on rocks, scrubby pines, the small, whitewashed houses appearing infrequently along the road. No wonder so many of the young people go away to sea, or to England or America to find work. She recalls Lydia and her cousin on the freighter, settled in Houston, the brother Michael in London. Not a lot of work for young people here, Emma realizes.

"Miss Crawford, what are we going to do about lunch?" Sam McGregor, the young physician in the group who works at Guy's Hospital in London setting broken bones, asks confidently.

Restored Drawing, Temple of Apollo, Bassae

Temple of Apollo, Bassae

Temple of Apollo, Bassae

He loves art history and spends his precious two weeks of holiday each year with Miss Crawford's touring group. Last year the group went to Spain. Emma has heard Miss Crawford is planning a trip to Tuscany next summer. Will Sam go along, she wonders idly, watching him.

"We'll arrive at the penultimate village before Bassae soon," the professor answers. "We'll be able to buy our picnic lunch there, then motor on to the site to eat it."

She smiles indulgently at Sam, a pet of sorts. Miss Crawford regards him as another professional like herself, and as a physician, he cannot be expected to know very much about art history. Her students, on the other hand, are held to a more exacting standard, thinks Emma somewhat resentfully, recalling how Miss Crawford lashes out at laziness, or what she describes as "sloppy thinking".

The Greek driver pulls up with a flourish at the center of a tiny village, simply a dot without a name on Emma's map, sending a few dispirited chickens running swiftly to safety, squawking with outrage. It is half-past eleven now and the sun is beginning to beat down mercilessly.

"We'll take time for a quick coffee," Miss Crawford calls out, indicating tables under trees at a small *taverna*. "Then you will have a few minutes to buy something for your lunch. There's a small provision store across the way." She point to a modest hut. "And farther up the hill in the village where the road narrows you will find a tiny kitchen selling delicious, hot, take-away items. But don't expect to find a Wimpy Bar and beef burgers!" She laughs heartily at her witticism.

Emma is certain Maria Crawford never ate a beef burger in her life. Food is absolutely unimportant to her. She's vaguely aware of what she eats, but only just. Painting and sculpture are her life, she cares for little else.

Yet Miss Crawford is scrupulous in halting at midmorning and afternoon to drink the strong Turkish coffee served everywhere in tiny cups. Emma likes this time for a break, time to relax, although she is not a serious coffee drinker.

Jane frowns at Emma and whispers, "I can just imagine what we'll find in that provision store over there. Nothing like shepherd's pie, or even a ploughman's lunch. It looks like a wind could blow the entire building over."

"It doesn't look very hopeful, I'll agree," says Emma, "but let's go and see."

The students climb down from the coach and approach the *taverna*. Jane and Emma move toward the store while their fellow students sink into the rickety chairs of the terrace and order coffee or limeade.

Inside, the provision store is dimly lit and feels cool. A screen door keeps out unwanted flying insects. Counter tops of linoleum look clean and well-scrubbed. Behind the old fashioned cash drawer, shelves gleam with brightly labeled tins of fruit and vegetables, presumably more in demand in winter. A table holds baskets of produce: tomatoes, eggplant, beans, oranges. To Emma it all looks fresh and inviting.

"Do you have any sandwiches?" Jane's voice is hopeful.

"No," came the reply from the woman shopkeeper. "But fresh yogurt and honey I can give," she says, smiling, showing even white teeth.

She wears a shapeless black dress covered by an immaculate white apron. They order two portions watching as the woman ladles the creamy yogurt into two small cartons and drizzles honey carefully over the top.

"You have spoons?" she asks and Emma nods. Both girls carry plastic utensils in their rucksacks.

"Good!" The woman's mouth widens in a bigger smile.

Emma realizes the woman is young. A matron, wearing the funereal black of an old woman. It is the same everywhere, at least in the villages Emma has seen, including Olympia. The apparent custom after marriage and motherhood requires women to wear black. Emma smiles at the woman, sighing inwardly. So unfair. And the Greek men she has noticed staring boldly at the girls in her group from *taverna* tables, nobody forces them into a premature old age. Many seem content to while away the hours sitting in front of the cafes while the wives work.

Jane takes stock as they make their way up the hill toward the take-away kitchen. "We've got some digestive biscuits left in our bags and an apple apiece. If we don't find anything else, we won't starve, Emma."

"Of course we won't, silly. But I'll bet we find something."

Searching for the tiny kitchen draws them onward, and they soon come upon a shop, sending forth delicious aromas which permeate the narrow road. It is only a small hut with no door; instead, a wide window at waist level opens onto the street with a ledge underneath which holds steaming pans of food.

"Fresh made *pastitsio* and *spanokopita*!" a woman calls out to them from inside. In the dim interior they see two women, one of them busily cleaning pans and bowls. But where is the oven? Emma peers into the corners but can see nothing.

Obviously their work for the day is almost finished, only the selling remains. Just two dishes to prepare, and when they are sold, down come the shutters over the opening.

Emma's mouth waters. The food looks delicious. They decide to buy one portion of each, and share. The *pastitsio* looks like a macaroni cheese dish, the *spanokopita* is a quiche, made with spinach, various cheeses and nutmeg as ingredients along with milk and eggs. The woman carefully lifts the warm, aromatic squares into two cartons with lids.

"Thank you," says Emma. "Pardon me, I was just wondering, where is your oven?"

"No oven here," the woman smiles, displaying a fine set of strong, white teeth. "Over there at the baker's. We use his ovens after the bread is finished baking. Everybody in village uses the baker's oven after he finish. We have no ovens in our houses." Jane and Emma look at her in amazement.

"I see," says Emma meekly, gaining a new insight into how people the world over manage their affairs in as many different ways. Travel is in some ways an humbling experience she realizes.

The students crowd onto the coach carrying parcels of cheese, fruit, bread and bottles of water. As the coach springs into life, the road soon narrows, turning into little more than a trail with few signs of human habitation. How did anyone ever make the journey to this remote place before the advent of motor transport? Much less, build a temple, thinks Emma as they jolt along.

Miss Crawford calls to them to look sharp for their first glimpse of Bassae. The coach rolls to a stop in a small clearing. No other coaches, no cars, no turnstiles, no attendants. Already they are falling under the magic spell of Bassae's charm. There are cries of wonder as they spot it above them, a survivor of many centuries, its deserted ruins standing solitary and majestic.

"We'll climb up to the site from here," Miss Crawford says, "And first we'll have our picnic among the ruins, then I'll give you my thoughts on the place. You are very privileged, you know, for few people know about Bassae, let alone make the difficult journey here. But I assure you, each one of you will never forget the experience. I can recall my first glimpse of Bassae as clearly as though it were yesterday."

Camera cases, notebooks and sun hats emerge, and carefully bearing their lunch parcels, the students begin the ascent. They follow an overgrown trail of sorts spangled with wild red poppies and yellow celandine growing among the rocks. The site is deserted, only the faint tinkling of the ever-present goat bells in the distance, majestic blue sky overlaid with fleecy clouds, the remaining columns of the Temple of Bassae thrusting upwards. Whispering winds play mischievously about. Voices soften as they enter the magic of Bassae, an experience to be stored carefully in memory's trunk.

A cluster of girls, looking like large butterflies in brightly colored cotton dresses, arrange themselves for their picnic around Sam, the young doctor, and Brian Gibbs, a photographer who is collaborating with Miss Crawford on a book about Greek art. The two unwittingly claim the title of most dazzling male members of the group, Sam with his shock of straight blond hair falling engagingly over his forehead; Brian, brown wavy hair and horn rimmed spectacles giving him the faintly Byronic air of the scholar.

They make no effort to seek out company, it rushes to them, Emma thinks waspishly, resolving that she will not pay court to either of them. Instead she takes out a tiny compact and glances at her windblown hair, blue eyes fixed disapprovingly on the tiny band of freckles lightly marching across her nose. She snaps the compact shut, giving full attention to her lunch, her friend Jane and the magnificent site before them.

Miss Crawford eats alone by choice, unless she decides on a whim to summon her friend Geneva or 'Gee' as she prefers to be called, for company. Gee is one of the students nearer in age to Professor Crawford. Occasionally Miss Crawford invites the Fenways to join her. None of the students would dare approach, unless summoned.

Lance Fenway, from the department of travel and foreign studies at London University, has the responsibility for making the tour run smoothly. He must arrange hotel rooms, see that luggage is collected and loaded on to the coach, arrange transport to the sites and find cheap *tavernas* serving filling food for their evening meal. No wonder Lance and Fiona Fenway cherish their few moments off duty, Emma reflects, for husband and wife remain at Miss Crawford's beck' and call every minute.

Emma and Jane sit away from the group, looking out over the valley below. The panorama they face is rocky, rugged and enchantingly beautiful, typical of the landscape of mountainous Greece.

Glancing to one side they can observe Miss Crawford perched on a flat rock, prim in brown poplin suit and white tailored blouse, dressed as though for a lecture in the British Museum. A straw sun hat hides dark, curly hair. Sensible brown walking shoes with low heels encase long, narrow feet.

"Looks every inch the lecturer, doesn't she?" Jane whispers, as she and Emma silently admire.

"Do you think it's true, that she never received a degree?" Emma's voice sounds incredulous. "And teaching at London University! I can hardly believe it!"

"It's true, all right. Her father was a distinguished professor at Cambridge and she was taught at home. She started sculpting when she was still in her 'teens, had a love affair, a brief one, with a famous art historian, and never found the time or the inclination to enroll in university. But all the while she was reading everything she could get her hands on, studying all the best art history writers. Richter, Panofsky, Wittkower, Burckhardt, you know, the unreadable ones. She started lecturing a little, free lance you see, when someone from the University happened to hear her and realized she is a living, breathing masterpiece herself! Lance's superiors pounced on her and, well, you know the rest."

"I know she is by far the most brilliant lecturer at the university, probably the most brilliant one I ever heard. What about her sculpting?"

"Went by the boards. She found she had a taste for lecturing and became obsessive about it. They want to make her head of extra-mural art history, so the rumor goes, but she's got to get her degree first. So far, she doesn't seem to be in any hurry. Likes what she's doing, and isn't ambitious." Jane grins at Emma.

Lunch finished, the students lift sun-starved faces to the sky, soaking up the warmth as well as the atmosphere of Bassae. They crave the sun so much Emma observes, looking around her, because it almost never shines in London. Wistfully she lets her thoughts wander back to Crozet, her home in Virginia. Not as sunny as Greece, perhaps, but more sun than London by a long sight. No wonder her father jumped at the chance of a professorship at the University of Virginia all those years ago. He packed his bags and left England for good. Soon after his arrival he met and married Emma's mother, a young teacher of psychology at the university.

Emma, named for her paternal grandmother, spent several wonderful summers at her cottage in Haslemere in Surrey before her grandmother, Emma Matilda, died. Unbidden, a few sepia stills spring to mind: tea in a shaded garden smelling of old roses in summer; her grandmother's book-lined library where she could curl up with Scott's Ivanhoe and lose herself in the dimly lit depths smelling faintly of lavender polish and old leather bindings; nocturnal mists of rain falling outside the window beside her bed.

Emma grew to love England and was overjoyed when she received a grant for a year of advanced study in London. She turns her face toward the sun, eyes closed, as she forwards to a dream of the future, perhaps lecturing at some world-famous museum.

Miss Crawford's brief talk at the site holds the group spellbound. In spite of eccentricity, she speaks superbly and the students are fiercely loyal even though they fear her random, stinging criticisms. She finishes by describing the vanished frieze inside the cella which had no doubt been the glory of the Temple of Apollo at Bassae.

"Fragments are on display in London, but in Oxford, at the Ashmolean Museum, this frieze of the battle of the Greeks and the Amazons has been reproduced in its entirety on the staircase wall. The museum was designed by C.R. Cockerell in 1845, after he visited Bassae in 1838-9. It obviously made a substantial impression. Cockerell used the unusual Corinthian column type from Bassae when he designed the museum's exterior front. I sincerely hope you will journey to Oxford this summer to view this unique tribute to Bassae."

The sun is beginning to sink in the sky and the driver Alexander gently touches her elbow, saying they should make for the coach.

"Roads are bad. We do not drive good in the dark," he explains.

"Ah, yes, Alexander," she answers, her manner expansive. "How right you are. Time to depart." And the group busily scrambles among the columns, snapping final photographs, gathering up water bottles and rucksacks, tidying up the site.

Suddenly the peace of the day is shattered by the appearance of a wild-looking shepherd wearing patched and faded trousers held up by a bit of rope around the waist, worn black shirt and shabby shoes without socks completing his attire. Shoulder length hair is speckled with grey, matted and uncombed, an unkempt beard covering the lower part of his face. Black eyes glare wildly under menacing overhanging brows. The thought flashes through Emma's mind that he looks like the figure of the troll living under the bridge in a Hans Christian Andersen fairy tale. He advances swiftly, frowning, raising both arms in a threatening gesture.

"You have taken it!" he cries in heavily accented English. "You have stolen one of our treasures!" Frozen into silence, members of the group stare blankly back at him.

Quickly Miss Crawford steps forward. Perfectly calm, she raises the furled umbrella she uses as a pointing stick, and confronts the man. Instinctively the students edge closer.

"The amulet! The amulet!" he cries. "It has been hidden safe in the hills for generations, for over two hundred years. And now it has been stolen and you have taken it. I know it! Guilt is written on your faces. The Apollo Amulet is missing!"

"My good man, we know nothing about what you are saying. None of these students nor I have the faintest idea of what you are talking about." Maria Crawford speaks calmly but with assured conviction as she surveys the man. The hermit, somewhat taken aback by her commanding presence, retreats a step.

"Now tell me precisely what you believe has been stolen," she demands, quickly pressing the advantage, her voice firm.

"Lady, it is the figure of Apollo carved on an amulet, the same figure this temple was built to honor. It is an amulet handed down generation after generation from father to son, a valuable amulet said to have been created by the famous sculptor Phidias himself, so legend has it. Handed down and down, then hidden in a secret place, near here, for safekeeping." He pauses, tugging at the rope belt at his waist, as though to emphasize his words.

"Recently the secret place was plundered. The amulet stolen. With my own eyes I saw the place where it was hidden; now it is empty."

A slight frown crosses Miss Crawford's brow. She thinks the man is deranged, but does not wish to antagonize him.

"If you will give me your name and the name of your village," she answers, taking a tiny notebook and pen from her pocket, "I will take down the information and make inquiries." Meekly he mumbles a rambling, disjointed reply as she listens intently.

"Is there anything more you wish to tell me?" She appears unhurried in manner as she makes notes, not wishing to set off any alarms in the mind of the troubled man.

"Lady, the Apollo Amulet has been hidden, buried, for many years. My plan was to dig it up and take it to the museum authorities in Athens. Such things should be on display for all to see."

Again he pauses, peering earnestly at her. She nods encouragingly. The man's face takes on a faraway, dreamy look. Miss Crawford's face is a study in sympathy.

"And someone has stolen it from you," she finishes softly, shaking her head. "I can understand how you thought a British group might have stolen it. After all, we took away your treasures from the Parthenon all those years ago. No matter how well-meaning the perpetrators of *that* operation were, it was wrong. But, my good man, these are only students with me, students come to pay homage to the glory that is Bassae! Someone else has stolen your treasure. And I can only promise you that I shall make inquiries when I get to Athens. I will do whatever I can to help and send word back to you of what I find out."

Calmer now, the man lowers his head, completely won over by her words and her demeanor. He mumbles his thanks, turns and disappears as quickly as he has come. The students begin filing silently toward the coach, disturbed by what they have seen. In the journey back to Olympia and the Pensione Anastasia they speak in whispers about the mysterious man. Although most of them believe he is mad, his story holds a certain ring of truth. An amulet placed in his care for safe keeping has been stolen.

"Maybe there truly *is* a long-lost amulet of Apollo by Phidias, wouldn't that be something?" whispers Jane to Emma. Miss Crawford sits silently, lost in her own thoughts.

Emma speculates on a different aspect of the recent drama which unfolded before their eyes on the heights of Bassae. Miss Crawford, while carefully avoiding mention of Lord Elgin, had clearly been thinking of his actions in a century long gone. The cornerstone of Greek national pride, sculptures from the ruin of the Parthenon, had been crated and shipped away in staggering numbers to England by Lord Elgin, a diplomat, where they remain even to this day. *And she was sympathetic to the idea of their return to Greece!* Emma gains a new respect and even greater admiration for their professor as she ponders her words to the Greek rustic, or shepherd, who accosted them.

But the wild herder who burst upon them at the temple ruins. What can he mean, has a famous Greek treasure been stolen? Or is it simply a fantasy being played out in his mind?

TWO

Disaster at the Temple of Zeus; an Accident at Delphi

The *taverna* chosen by Lance Fenway for their evening meal is two streets away from the Pensione Anastasia. Paper lanterns strung in the trees in front and tables placed underneath give the restaurant a festive air, disguising its humble origins.

The tables are fashioned of simple planks resting on sawhorses and covered with coarse white paper. Benches are placed on the sides. Already townspeople are gathering: young couples with children, elderly parents, toddlers playing tag in and around the tables, a few dogs. A three-piece band starts tuning up on the *taverna* porch. A celebration of some local festival appears to be on the horizon.

Jane, Emma and the other students are caught up in the excitement. The local priest wearing the clerical hat of the Eastern church and long black robes set off by a large silver cross hanging from his neck, weaves in and out of the crowd, pausing to give greetings, words of comfort. He stops to chat with Miss Crawford, who sits surrounded by students.

"What is the celebration in honor of, Father?" she inquires.

"Only an early observance of May Day. We have a number of festivities during this season. It means to us that spring, a time of renewal, is upon us." He smiles benignly as he makes his way through the clusters of tables, patting children on the head, embracing the men of the village, pausing to speak a few words to the elderly, chatting in a jovial manner with both young mothers and grandmothers.

He really knows them and cares for them, Emma thinks, watching the lively scene before her. She tries to imagine herself living in such a village, swathed in black like the women, perhaps managing the family provision store while her husband drinks coffee with the men in the shade of the trees in front of the *taverna*. But her imagination is unequal to the task. For all its simplicity and charm, life in a village in Greece holds only a limited appeal. She recalls the village near Bassae, only one oven for the entire village!

"You're looking lovely tonight, Emma," a voice behind her says. Quickly she turns. Lance Fenway, so thoroughly polite and forthright, his remark strikes her for just what it is, a sincere compliment.

"Thank you, Lance. Fiona looks wonderful in her blue dress."

"I think so too. I chose it for her." He gazes fondly at his wife, sitting with Gee, Miss Crawford and Sam at the next table.

"Emma," he speaks quietly into her ear, turning slightly away from Jane who is talking with Brian Gibbs. "The *taverna* has only one entree tonight, barbecued goat. I think we should be careful to refer to it only as 'barbecue' don't you? Some in our group might be a bit squeamish if they knew otherwise, don't you think?" He smiles, giving a slight lifting of his brow and the suggestion of a nod in Jane's direction. Emma swallows painfully. Barbecued or not, goat meat is not at the top of her list, but she cannot let Lance down.

"Of course," she answers, "Count on me."

When everyone is seated the waiters bring out individual salad bowls containing wedges of tomato, chunks of goat cheese, wrinkled, briny black olives and fresh lettuces, all tossed in olive oil with a little vinegar and lemon juice. There is *retsina*, the resin-flavored wine of Greece and liter bottles of the universal coca cola. The *taverna* owner proudly presents them with complimentary bottles of fizzy water for their table. Emma notes that these refinements do not extend to tables where the villagers sit. They drink only *retsina* or the water from the communal village wells. Lance obviously has ordered alternative beverages for the party from London.

The main course arrives at the moment the band begins playing in earnest, drowning out all attempts at conversation. Pieces of heavy butcher's paper fashioned into pouches are brought out, holding individual portions of delicious smelling meat and a generous serving of fried potatoes, What a neat way of serving, Emma thinks, peering at the succulent food placed before her.

"Oh, dear," murmurs Jane nervously, looking anxious. "What is it?"

"Barbecue," Emma replies, taking a pinch between her fingers and putting it in her mouth. "It tastes delicious. You'll like it, Jane," Emma tells her, feeling only the tiniest twinge of conscience. After all, as Lance said, it is barbecue, and everyone knows Jane is suspicious of unknown food when she travels abroad.

"The chips are heavenly, Jane. Almost as good as those at the Gower Street Cafe in London."

Emma cannot understand the British students' craving for fried potatoes, chips, they call them. They eat them repeatedly and never seem to show an ounce of weight. It must be all the walking required in a big city, walking to the bus, to the underground, walking for the pleasure of it. London traffic snarls are legendary and a motor car in the inner city can be an enormous handicap, making much less sense than walking or cycling.

After they finish the meal with *baklava*, thin pastry layers laced with nuts and honey, Emma watches Miss Crawford lead the Fenways, Gee, Brian and Sam to a section of the road in front of them roped off for dancing. An unbroken line of dancers perform maneuvers of the dance to the accompaniment of a thwanging guitar, a *bouzouki*, and a clarinet. Around and around the dancers twirl; faster and faster, music pounding.

Miss Crawford joins the line. Extremely light on her feet, she looks cool and dignified in a white dress of Greek design, simple, straight cut with magnificent pleated sleeves accented with lace insets. She dances with complete concentration and abandon, giving herself to the swaying, studied motions. Not surprisingly she is the undisputed belle of the evening. Sam and the others follow her, somewhat woodenly at first, but her grace and sure steps guide them like a beacon. The villagers applaud. Sam makes his way to the table where Jane and Emma are seated, watching the dancers.

"Come now. Time for you both to take to the floor."

"Oh, I really couldn't," Jane's face holds a look of horror. "You two go on."

"Rubbish. It won't do, Jane. I'll show you." Sam is determined.

And grasping their hands, he pulls both girls to their feet and hustles them toward the dancers. Emma loves dancing and studied ballet as a child. She moves smoothly with the music. And with Sam's encouragement, Jane catches on quickly and is soon swaying to the wailing rhythms. Emma notices that while many of the village men join the line of dancers, the women remain at their tables with younger children and elderly parents. Only the young, unmarried girls join the dance.

When Miss Crawford steps out of the line around midnight, it signals the end of the evening, and the students began drifting toward Pensione Anastasia. Emma finds herself walking with Sam.

"An unforgettable evening," Sam says, taking her arm to guide her around a group of sleepy children being nudged homeward by their parents.

"It must be a tremendous release to get away from such demanding work at the hospital. Have you been to Greece before?" Emma asks.

"This trip is a life line for me," he says simply. "No, I've never been here before, have you?"

Emma shakes her head, wondering what she can say next. Seldom at a loss for words, she is amazed at her shyness and gropes for a conversational limb to grasp as they stroll; she feels as though she has been stricken dumb.

"What did you think of the man who appeared at Bassae today?" Sam asks.

"Oh, the shepherd," says Emma. "I feel terribly sorry for him, he expressed such deep sadness of pain and loss. He believes what he told us. I'm just not quite sure he is living in the real world. Certainly his is a world different from ours."

Sam nods. "That's what I felt. His words held the ring of truth, but on the other hand, he could be delusional. How did you think Crawford handled it?"

"She was very, very good. Did you see how she took charge from the first? And she won him over completely. She was cool and composed. If I end up being a lecturer, I hope I can be half as collected as she. Do you really suppose she'll check out his story? And report back to him?" Emma's voice holds admiration and awe.

"Yes, I believe she will. It wasn't just an act. I believe she is genuinely interested in the poor guy. You know, for all her eccentricities, she's straight as an arrow; honest, I mean, and she doesn't give her word lightly. Those remarks she made about the Parthenon sculptures clearly came from the heart. She believes they should be returned to Greece. She told us earlier tonight that she had heard of the legend of the Apollo Amulet, heard it the first time she ever came to the Arcadian hills of Bassae when she was a lot younger. So it is a legend people have known about for many years. But only a legend."

They walk on in silence for a few minutes, absorbing the beauty of the night around them. "And what do you hope to gain from these two weeks in Greece, Emma?" His tone is light, half-joking.

Emma looks him straight in the eye. "A better understanding of Greek temples and sculpture for a start, a foundation in Greek art before I leave the UK to go home and find a curatorial post or possibly teach somewhere."

She speaks calmly, her face blank like an unpainted canvas, giving nothing away. She keeps her voice matter of fact. *Even though you are attractive, I will not join your feminine cheering section. You'll have to get along without me in the chorus.*

"I see. And if you fall in love with England and decide you want to stay?" his voice trails off and she finds herself to her horror pretending he really means 'someone' not 'England.'

Emma looks calmly at Sam. "Yes, I suppose I could decide to stay. My father is British. I spent several summers visiting my grandmother in Surrey before she died, so living here is something I've experienced before. But," she finishes brightly, "I don't think I will."

They walk, lost in their own thoughts, to the Pensione Anastasia entry before Sam speaks again. "So sure of yourself, so self-possessed. I admire you, Miss Emma Darling," and quickly he plants a kiss on the top of her head then guides her firmly inside. Emma hurries upstairs to her room, heart pounding in spite of herself.

"A good evening?" Jane asks when Emma enters the room.

Jane, in pajamas, turns down the covers of her bed. Removing her headband, she takes up a brush and begins brushing her hair until it shines like a cap of darkened gold.

"A very good evening," Emma answers softly and begins to prepare for bed, thoughts of Sam crowding unbidden into her head.

From the open window, down the road at the *taverna*, strains of music from the restaurant float toward her as the dancing continues. Indeed Emma can faintly hear music drifting in long after midnight when she drops at last into a deep sleep, untroubled by dreams.

~

Jane has already left for breakfast when Emma awakes. Quickly she dresses and hurries downstairs. A free morning. The group is to meet at the nearby Temple of Zeus after lunch. The dining room is deserted. She sinks down into a chair, still feeling sleepy. Lydia hurries over to her with the coffee and milk jugs, a wide smile on her face.

"Good morning, Miss. Coffee for you?" Emma nods and Lydia pours the steaming liquids from both pitchers into Emma's cup, then stands uncertainly, first on one foot, then on the other. She appears unable to leave.

"Is something on your mind, Lydia?" Emma asks.

"Miss," she blurts out. "My mother has made *baklava* for my brother's birthday, my brother Michael who is in London. He loves her *baklava* very much. I was wondering, could you take the package back to him in London?"

Impulsively Emma smiles, prepared to say that she will be glad to take the package. Then, inexplicably, bells go off in her head. She remembers warnings from the check-in counter at Heathrow, warnings to passengers not to carry wrapped packages on board for anyone, friend or stranger.

A small voice inside speaks, "You shouldn't offer to do this, Emma, not even something seemingly harmless like a package of *baklava*."

Emma hesitates then says firmly, "I'm sorry, Lydia, but I really can't do that. Couldn't you mail it?"

Lydia's face turns red and she hurries away, murmuring something about how she can manage very well without any suggestions and why some people in this world are selfish and care nothing for anyone but themselves.

Emma shrugs, but does not allow self-doubts to nag at her. It is not something thinking persons do, carry packages on airplanes for other people, strangers at that. If she has made an enemy of Lydia she is sorry, but it cannot be helped.

At that moment Sam appears in the deserted dining room and sits down beside her with news from Jane, whom he's seen at the market. Jane sends word that she will meet Emma after lunch at the Temple of Zeus, after she finishes shopping. Emma quietly relates to Sam the entire episode with Lydia.

"You did the right thing, Emma. It's too risky and dangerous to take anything belonging to someone else. A plane could be blown up; at the very least customs might uncover something unpleasant, goodness knows what, in that *baklava*."

~

Slowly Emma and Sam make their way over to the ruins of the Temple of Zeus to meet the others. Though the ruins are fragmentary after centuries of plundering, good records remain and placement of columns has been restored. After an introductory talk by Miss Crawford they move into the adjacent Olympia Museum. Small, dim, fusty, it holds wonderful fragments of sculptures from the pediments of the temple as well as careful reconstruction of other figures. A clay figure group of Zeus carrying off the child Ganymede who holds a cock, the usual Greek love gift for a boy, bears traces of bright color. Many works were painted during the period of fifth century BC. Maria Crawford describes the sculptures with great sensitivity and understanding.

Jane has joined Emma, thrilled with her purchases of a white cotton drawstring blouse and a multicolored leather coin purse for her mother. "The blouse will be perfect to wear in London with summer skirts," she whispers, "if it ever warms up and we have a summer."

As the group clusters around her in the darkened room, Maria Crawford begins describing the beautiful pediment sculptures in the severe style, showing the Battle of the Lapiths and the Centaurs at the wedding feast.

"The Lapiths are warriors, the centaurs half man, half horse. This design covers the west pediment." Miss Crawford begins. "A brawl commences when the centaurs, who have become drunk, begin to cart off not only the bride, but all of the other Lapith women as well. The figure of Apollo in the center is meant to symbolize the rule of law. Clearly, the Lapiths of Thessaly are in the right here, not the unkempt, uncouth centaurs, who never learned at their mothers' knees how to behave in polite company.

"Switching to the other exterior end of the temple, the pediment over the main, or east entrance contains the figure of Zeus in the center, with participants of the chariot race ranged rather woodenly on either side. However, it is a static and lifeless composition, compared to the battle scene on the west pediment which I've just described.

Restored Drawing, Temple of Zeus, Olympia.

Clay Sculpture Zeus and Ganymede, Olympia Museum

Reconstructed Sculpture, Lapith Woman. Olympia Museum

"Within the *cella*, or inner room of this temple stood the magnificent chryselephantine, that is, gold and ivory, statue of Zeus by the great sculptor Phidias. Zeus was seated, with a figure of Victory held in his outstretched right palm. The statue was stolen and taken to Constantinople at some point where it was destroyed by fire in 475 AD, but in a small, precious accident of fate, a tea mug belonging to the great Phidias was uncovered here on the site at Olympia in 1954 by archeologists. It bears the inscription, "I belong to Phidias" on its base. So we know Phidias was on the site working."

Suddenly Jane speaks out, looking up from her guide book, "But Miss Crawford, the guidebook says these sculpture fragments we are looking at are reconstructions." As soon as she utters the words her eyes widen in fear. She realizes she had done the unthinkable: corrected the lecturer in front of the entire group.

Retribution is both swift and cruel. "And since you are the authority, Miss Hale, tell us please about the style in which these sculptures are created, the severe style. Give us dates, please."

Maria Crawford's voice is icy. Two red spots burning in her cheeks tell the students Jane must be right; the lecturer had omitted the fact that the fragments are reconstructions. Faces of the students transform into chalky, unreal masks, frozen in apprehension. Emma holds her breath.

Poor Jane, Emma's heart breaks for her. She babbles incoherently in a stricken voice, trying to respond with conviction, but finally the voice stills to a whisper as silence in the little museum hangs like a shroud on the air. Miss Crawford turns away and carries on with her talk as though Jane does not exist. When she has finished, she dismisses the group, walking quickly out of the room, leaving the students standing awkwardly about in embarrassed silence. Taking Jane's arm, Emma hurries with her to the Anastasia.

Later, Emma hears other students returning to the Pensione Anastasia and a few of the girls knock timidly on Jane and Emma's door to murmur about the unfairness of the outburst by their lecturer.

"Jane was really right, you know," they whisper, but Jane is inconsolable.

Her tender nature has been bruised. She can only lie, head buried in her pillow, pretending sleep. Later, long after the group finishes dinner without her, Jane continues to lie on her bed, feigning sleep. Emma is achingly aware of her muffled, pillow sobs late into the night.

~

Emma, awake early in the semi-darkness of pre-dawn, realizes Jane finally has drifted into a troubled sleep. She slides quietly out of bed and goes to the window, looking out at the barren, rocky slopes in the distance beginning to turn faintly pink with the arrival of dawn. A few scrubby pines dot faraway hillsides. Beyond the Pensione Anastasia she sees the carefully terraced rows of olive trees. The ever-present scent of rosemary perfumes the early morning air. How I'll miss Greece when we leave, she thinks, momentarily forgetting to worry about Jane.

Leaning on her window ledge, she hears muted voices below, coming from the kitchen. Surely it is too early for breakfast preparations to begin. Miss Crawford has declared eight o'clock as their breakfast time, and there are no other guests at the pensione. The approaching voices grow louder, angry men arguing in Greek. Emma strains to hear and to see.

Suddenly the door to the kitchen flies open and two men barge into the small courtyard, a service area below her window. The larger man seems to be threatening the smaller one. With a start Emma makes out the features of the Bassae Shepherd. She recognizes him as he edges away from the tall man whom Emma has also seen before. He is Lydia's father, the pensione owner. His arm is upraised as though about to strike the shepherd.

What on earth? Emma frowns as the Bassae Shepherd disappears around the side of the building. Bassae is many kilometers away. What business can the shepherd possibly have here? He must have been trying to speak to Miss Crawford, but Emma discards this idea almost immediately. He wouldn't have come to seek out Miss Crawford before dawn, now would he? The anger of the two men indicates a much more sinister encounter. Somehow, Emma has a hunch it relates to the missing Apollo Amulet. But how? The roseate hue of the sky deepens; Jane is stirring.

"Get up, Lazybones, you can have first crack at that luxury bath down the hall if you hurry." Emma's voice is teasing. She fervently hopes Jane's even-tempered equilibrium has returned.

The Greek bathtub is a private joke between them, so small they must draw up their knees under their chins to sit in it, and the erratic water supply drips in fitful trickles or spurts in great gushes.

"I think I'll stay in bed," Jane mumbles, avoiding Emma's eyes. Emma sits on the side of her bed.

"No you don't, Jane, you're not going to let this defeat you, not if I can help it. Miss Crawford is the villain in this drama. You were right, Jane, you were right! Don't you remember how people stopped by the room last night, giving you their support? Besides, you don't want to miss going to Delphi today, do you? We'll be seeing the Delphi Charioteer."

"But Miss Crawford will make me feel miserable." Jane's face mirrors a picture of despair.

"No she won't. She knows she came down on you too hard. She'll ease off. Just give her a chance." Jane looks down at her bitten fingernails and sighs as Emma speaks up in her defense.

"You're right, Emma, as usual. I can't stay in bed forever like a slug. But oh how I hate to face everyone." She swings legs over the side of the bed and reaches for her sponge bag. "I'll go battle with that bathtub."

When Emma tells Jane what she saw and heard at the window earlier, Jane agrees the men must have been talking about the amulet. But what could it all mean? As the girls go downstairs for breakfast, Sam is waiting.

"It's our last night in Greece before we fly out from Athens tomorrow evening. Some of the girls are planning to have dinner together, Jane, and they want you to join them." He turns toward Emma.

"Emma, I'd like for you to have dinner with me."

He's checked everything out, thinks Emma, looking at Jane's beaming face. And Jane's face tells her she wants to be with the group.

"I'd love to go with you, Sam. It's hard to realize the trip is almost finished. Just tomorrow in Athens, then Heathrow will be the next stop." All at once Emma feels a surge of happiness. Does being with Sam mean all that much? Apparently so, she decides, dismissing her feelings as silly.

The coach reaches the outskirts of Delphi, along with a fleet of motor cars decked out with wreaths of May Day flowers and streamers. Alexander, the driver, confirms the occasion heralds the arrival of spring and is celebrated with great enthusiasm all over Greece. Students crowd the windows of the coach, snapping photographs of young girls sitting on car bonnets, tossing blossoms to pedestrians who cheer and clap their hands.

The red bud, or Judas trees are in blossom, masses of pink flowers like crepe paper rosettes adding festivity to the cavalcade. Emma knows that Delphi, home of the Oracle, the Temples of Apollo and Athena Pronaea, and the Amphitheater, has been a revered, holy place for many centuries.

They make their way to the museum. In the center of the modest room stands the bronze Delphi Charioteer, his chariot now lost, almost life-size, the crowning achievement of the archaic age, by an unknown sculptor. Emma studies the figure, wearing the long pleated dress of the chariot rider, hair bound in place by a gleaming gold filet and eyes of stone and glass, so lifelike they startle her. She expels a small sigh of admiration heard only by Jane standing beside her.

Temple of Apollo, Delphi

Charioteer, Delphi Museum, C.470 BC

Amphitheater and Temple of Apollo, Delphi

"He would have been displayed outdoors in the burning sun of Greece in the ancient world, accompanied by a groom and horses, now lost. What an impressive sight he would have been," Jane breathes reverently.

"The piece actually celebrates the Olympic games of 478 BC. Can you believe it, Emma? That the Olympics had already begun, way back then?" Jane goes on to say that originally, the filet would have been made of silver, the charioteer's lips of copper.

The group begins gathering around the sculpture, silently studying it for some minutes, waiting for Miss Crawford. The image is a familiar one to all of them, having seen reproductions in art books, but seeing the actual figure produces a respectful silence.

"It's like seeing a dream," sighs Jocelyn, the romantically minded young matron from Surrey. "It's so much larger than I'd thought."

"He looks vibrant, alive," Jane adds softly. "We're seeing him breathe; I expect him to speak and think."

"Very perceptive, Miss Hale," Miss Crawford's voice flows over them, clarion tones filling every atom of space in the tiny exhibition room. She is standing behind Jane, who whirls quickly around as her face turns red as a tomato, but she looks tremendously pleased. Inwardly Emma relaxes. Miss Crawford cannot bring herself to apologize, tell Jane she was right that they *were* looking at reproductions in the Olympia Museum, but in her way she is trying to make amends for the fiasco of yesterday.

After speaking to them briefly about the charioteer, Miss Crawford consults the small watch held to her wrist by a slim black ribbon band. "All right now, it is almost one o'clock and time to break for lunch. I am scheduled to meet a former colleague, here at the museum, so we will go our separate ways. You may find lunch in the town, or picnic here in the museum grounds. Just be back at the museum at two-thirty sharp and Alexander will drive you to the site. While you are there, you will want to look over all the ruins, temples, treasury and of course the amphitheater. You'll be on your own this afternoon. Just be at the coach set down point by four p.m. to return to Pensione Anastasia in Olympia. Don't be late."

"You won't be lecturing on the site, Miss Crawford?" Primrose Wise speaks up, in a whining tone, a small, owl-like girl with glasses thick as wine bottle bottoms. She always looks as though her nearest and dearest relative has just died.

"No, Primrose, I have business I must attend to after lunch. I must make some telephone calls to Athens. My plan is to join you at the coach at four and then you can tell me what you have seen and observed on your own. I expect some thoughtful and perceptive comments, mind."

The lecturer leaves them abruptly and Primrose, all hope abandoned, makes for the amphitheater on foot while the rest of the group prepares for their picnic lunch.

Jane and Emma exchange glances. Could those telephone calls Miss Crawford mentioned pertain to the Bassae Shepherd and the Apollo Amulet? The two of them decide to walk the short distance into Delphi, a village about the size of Olympia, buy picnic provisions, then return to the museum grounds to eat lunch.

Under the shade of blossoming red bud trees whose flowers seem to stain the blue sky over their heads into a rich salmon color, the two girls eat in silence, overlooking the deep gorge behind the museum. As a temple site, Delphi possesses all the mystique and romance of Bassae, yet it is not nearly so remote, Emma reflects. From their picnic spot they can see tourists everywhere, scrambling over the ruined site, wearing sun hats, burdened with cameras.

After the break for lunch, the group boards the coach for the short distance to the temple and amphitheater sites, promising Alexander to be on time for a four o'clock pickup as they disembark. They trudge off toward the ruins, scattering into groups of twos and threes.

The sun beats down on them in all of its midday power and Emma envies Alexander, who can hardly wait to see them off the coach to settle down in the driver's seat, cover his face with a newspaper and prepare to take a long nap, cozy and cool, parked in the shade of a large, spreading Judas tree.

"Let's go to the amphitheater ruins first," Jane suggests.

They are standing at the bottom of the ruined amphitheater bending over their guidebook, trying to work out dimensions when a piercing cry rings out. It is short and sharp, a cry of pain. Afraid it might be one of their group, they hurry upward and come upon a cluster of students huddled around Gee, who is sitting on a step, moaning and holding her foot.

Cries of "What happened?" and "What's the matter?" come from all sides.

"I stepped down into a little drainage channel or something, caught my foot and fell," Gee whimpers. "My foot hurts terribly. I'm afraid something may be broken. I, I can't walk." Her face looks greenish and her eyes open wide. She struggles to keep back tears.

Suddenly Sam appears, hurrying down from the top tier of the amphitheater ruins. He quickly bends over Gee and eases her foot out of the shoe. He touches the foot with the gentleness of a mother handling her newborn child, pressing slightly, all the while eyes never leaving Gee's round, slightly red face framed by unruly grey hair. He probes, looking for broken bones. Gee winces in pain in spite of his careful touch, but she does not cry out.

"I'm not certain, but it looks like there may be a broken bone. We'll have to get you to a doctor for an X-ray." He turns to Brian who has joined the little group.

"Brian, help me lift her. We'll make a seat of sorts with our arms and carry her to the coach. That will be quickest. Gee, put your arms around our shoulders and hold on. We won't drop you."

A somewhat silent, dispirited group watches as the coach rolls away taking Gee, Brian and Sam to the museum where colleagues of Miss Crawford can direct them to the nearest doctor's surgery in Delphi.

"Don't worry." Brian calls out to them through the open window of the coach as it pulls off. "She's going to be all right. Just go ahead and look at everything. It's your only chance to see Delphi. Alexander will be back at four as planned to pick you up. I promise."

Emma recalls how quickly and quietly Sam sized up the situation and took charge. Her admiration for Sam grows.

~

Later that afternoon the students arrive by coach at Pensione Anastasia, driven by Alexander, but Gee, Miss Crawford, Brian and Sam have not yet returned from the doctor's surgery.

Jane and Emma use the minutes before dinner to pack, since departure for Athens will be early. Jane finishes first.

"At last! I'm all done except for my rucksack, my handbag and the clothes I'm wearing tomorrow."

"What about the dress for tonight?" Emma asks.

"No problem. I can fit it in at the top of my case along with my pajamas. I left a little bit of room. Poor Gee, I do hope she's going to be all right. Such rotten luck. Did you see how ghastly her face looked? All grey. I, I guess I am not the only one on this trip with bad luck dogging their heels."

"It's the absolute bottom for Gee," Emma agrees. "Still, at least it's the end of the trip, not the beginning. She could have been out of commission for a lot longer. It could have happened at Corinth, or at the theater at Mycenae. Didn't Sam do a splendid job, taking charge like that?"

Jane smiles her approval. She knows I like Sam, Emma muses, studying her room-mate's open face.

Jane locks her case and places it on top of the wardrobe. Emma, whose packing isn't finished, leaves her case open on the bed. Arm in arm they go downstairs to be with the others and to wait. Time for dinner arrives and still they haven't returned.

Some students at the suggestion of Lance Fenway begin to drift off in small groups toward the *taverna*. Emma is left in the reception area with Lance and Fiona to await the return of Gee, Brian, Sam and Miss Crawford. Within a few minutes they arrive in a taxi, Gee pale, exhausted, tottering awkwardly on unfamiliar crutches, her foot in a solid-looking cast.

"What about dinner, Gee?" asks Lance.

"No, please. I couldn't eat. I only want to get into bed and rest." Fiona stands up, goes quickly to Gee's side and takes her arm.

"I'll get you in bed and tuck you in," she says soothingly. "Brian, why don't you have the kitchen send up soup and some milk. She says she isn't hungry, but a little food would be good for her."

"You are right. She must have something nourishing, like soup. That would be perfect," Sam speaks up quickly. "You had a nasty shock to your system, Gee, and your body needs nourishment, something light. I've given you a mild sedative so you'll sleep well." He turns toward Emma.

Sam speaks briefly to her then hurries upstairs for a fresh shirt. Emma, anticipating the evening ahead, looks sadly after Gee and Fiona as they slowly make their way upstairs to Gee's room.

~

"Will Gee be all right?" Emma asks as she and Sam leave the Pensione and stroll toward the *taverna*.

"First rate in four to six weeks. But she did break a small bone and she needs that cast. She'll manage fine with crutches." Why are doctors always so cheerful in the face of disaster, Emma wonders, thinking of poor Gee straining to maneuver the crutches, but she knows Sam is right not to brood.

"What a day it's been," Emma sighs, telling Sam about the early morning argument she heard below her window. Sam listens thoughtfully, asking her if she is sure about the identity of the Bassae Shepherd.

"Positive," she replies. "You remember the old bit of rope he used as a belt? It was the same, and he's an unusually small man. I remembered that too."

"You won't believe this," Sam says, "but I also saw the Bassae Shepherd today. He was at the doctor's dispensary in Delphi where we took Gee. He was complaining, claiming someone had pushed rocks down on him from a ledge overhanging the road near Delphi. He kept repeating that he was the last one in his family line and he was honor bound to recover the amulet to pass it on to his country. Then he claimed someone is trying to kill him. He managed to get out of the way and escape the rocks with only a cut on his arm which the doctor treated.

"I wish Miss Crawford had been with us. She could have asked him for more information. She was busy on the telephone most of the afternoon, I found out later, talking to the Athens police." Emma registers all that Sam has said, wondering how her observations in the pre-dawn below her window will fit into the puzzle of the missing amulet.

"The doctor told me that rumors are flying around Delphi that an important artifact has been uncovered in the Bassae area, something of great value, and the police know about it and are determined to keep it from leaving the country." Sam pauses thoughtfully.

"But surely all works of art are prohibited by law from leaving Greece," Emma says, her mind racing. "They remember the Parthenon sculptures."

"Of course, but remember, thieves aren't interested in working within the law. They're looking for a way to sneak it out, maybe in a package of *baklava*, what? And an amulet is easier to deal with than gigantic sculptures!" He smiles mischievously at Emma. "Just how big is an amulet, anyway?" Her eyes widen in spite of herself.

"You don't really think," she begins.

Sam shakes his head and smiles. "I'm only teasing you."

"Maybe Lydia is being used by the thieves," Emma replies. "Her father was the one talking to the shepherd, remember?" Suddenly the possibility of real danger looms up like a phantom. That such a conspiracy could possibly involve her seems frightening, yet if indeed a valuable amulet is missing, what is the first thing the thieves would do? Get it out of the country to a place with a sophisticated art market, say London, in an unsuspecting tourist's case, disguised in a harmless package of *baklava*. It's more than possible! Anxiously she expresses her fears to Sam.

"We don't know for sure, of course." Sam replies. "We are just letting our imagination wander. There are bound to be ways of getting something small out of the country. We're in the dark as to what they'll try. No need to panic until we find out more."

As the evening unfolds Emma learns that Sam comes from Edinburgh and studied at St. Andrews University in Scotland. His dream is to return to Scotland to practice medicine in a small town somewhere near Edinburgh. Because student grants in Britain are mingy and small, it has been a struggle for Sam's parents to send him to medical school. He feels a strong sense of responsibility for his two younger brothers and feels bound to help if either or both of them want to try for medical school.

"I want them to have the same chance I had," he says thoughtfully, watching the festive crowd at the *taverna* as the music falls in whines and waves around them.

Sam asks Emma more about life in Virginia. Has she ever visited Monticello, Thomas Jefferson's home?

"There's not a school child in Virginia who could escape it, even if she wished," Emma smiles, describing for him the rolling hills of Albemarle County near Charlottesville, her home at nearby Crozet, telling him about the rural beauty of Thomas Jefferson's Monticello, his gardens for both flowers and vegetables, his ingenious designs for furniture incorporated into the rooms of the historic and beautiful estate.

Emma discovers she likes Sam's company very much. She admires him for taking things slowly, for thinking before he speaks. And she silently applauds his commitment to his younger brothers.

I do believe he is a tortoise, not a hare, she reflects. Someone who deliberates before acting. But someone who can act quickly in a crisis, she amends, thinking of how quickly and efficiently he dealt with Gee's misfortune. She is firmly convinced there is indeed much to admire about Sam McGregor.

THREE

Death on Constitution Square. Or Is It Murder?

As she returns to her room, Emma notes with dismay the unfinished packing on her bed, just where she left it all those hours ago. She had forgotten it. Quickly she transfers her case to the floor, resolves to awake early and finish the job in the morning. She undresses quietly, steps into pajamas and sinks into bed, hoping she will not wake Jane who is sleeping soundly.

Morning brings the usual chaos of departure, feverish packing, transferring of cases to the hallway where they will be picked up and loaded onto the coach.

"Emma, remember the scarf I borrowed from you the first night? I found it just now at the back of my drawer. Can I put it in your case?"

"It's already locked, I'm afraid. If I open it, I may not be able to close it again. Why don't you keep it?"

"Oh no, I couldn't," Jane answers. "What if I tuck it into the little zipper pouch on the outside of your case?"

"Good idea!" Emma replies from the hallway, hurrying down to breakfast. Jane quickly stuffs the wisp of blue chiffon into the pouch and follows her.

Gee's breakfast is taken to her on a tray while Fiona packs her case. Then Brian and Sam carefully carry her down the stairs to conserve her energy and she makes her way to the coach using the crutches. She sits in the first seat behind the driver, across the aisle from Miss Crawford. Her cast elevated, she looks rested and ready for the long journey home after a day of sightseeing in Athens.

Lance oversees the loading of the luggage, then the coach slowly rolls away from Pensione Anastasia bound for Athens. As they leave, Emma recalls she has not seen Lydia since she refused to carry the *baklava*. She regrets she made an enemy, but it can't be helped. Once they are underway, Miss Crawford stands, faces the group, microphone in hand.

"I would normally have spoken to you in the dining room, but we were running a bit late. Also, some of what I have to say to you is of a confidential nature. First of all, I am happy to report that Gee is feeling comfortable after a restful night. We owe a lot to Sam for acting so quickly and competently on her behalf. By getting her to the museum, we were able to transfer her by motor to a nearby doctor's surgery and dispensary immediately. It is always a good idea to have a competent surgeon in our group, especially when visiting hilly museum sites." She smiles at her little joke.

"You all know our plans for Athens, so I shall add only the reminder that your baggage is now locked in the luggage compartment and will remain locked until we reach Athens airport where it will be transferred to our plane. You will not be permitted to retrieve it until we have landed at Heathrow tonight. This is a precaution ordered by the Athens police yesterday because of information they have learned."

The students look at one another registering surprise and the buzz of whispering floats up and down the coach. It quickly dies down as Miss Crawford resumes.

"Now, since our visit to Bassae I have been making inquiries about the lost amulet of Apollo which we were told about by the shepherd who accosted us there. It appears that such an amulet is recorded as having been in existence in ancient times. It has long been lost, and is something of a legend in that part of Arcadia surrounding the Bassae temple.

"Rumors have been circulating that the amulet has been found and stolen from its centuries-old hiding place in the hills near Bassae, and that an attempt will be made to get it out of the country and offer it for sale on the underground art market of stolen antiquities. That is why your luggage will be guarded so carefully.

"This of course is reprehensible. No reputable dealer or curator would even think of acquiring such a piece." Here Miss Crawford's brow wrinkles with displeasure. "It would have to appeal to unsavory individuals with more money than scruples who would be content to own such a treasure in secret. Unfortunately, there are people in this world who are willing to commit such a dishonorable act."

Emma smiles to herself. To Maria Crawford, art theft obviously represents the most heinous of crimes, surpassing mayhem and murder. Miss Crawford continues.

"Now I have attempted to reach the man we call the Bassae Shepherd by telephone, but apparently there is no telephone exchange near the area where he lives. So I have written a letter to him informing him that the police are aware of his problem and are taking every precaution to locate the thieves and retrieve the missing amulet. The Athens Inspector of Police urged me to tell you all that under no circumstances should you offer or consent to carry a package, no matter how small, back to London. If you have been approached by anyone, let me know at once." She pauses to look up and down the coach.

"Miss Crawford," Emma speaks up, "The day before yesterday, Lydia, the daughter of the owner of Pensione Anastasia, asked me to take a package of *baklava* back to her brother in London. It was baked by her mother, for his birthday. I didn't think it was important at the time.

"Now, after what you've just said, I realize I should have told you about it."

"And you refused to carry the package?" Miss Crawford asks quickly.

"Yes, I hated to refuse because it sounds harmless, but I told her I couldn't do it, that all air passengers are warned not to carry packages for anyone. I had a funny feeling about the request, nothing I could put my finger on, just a hunch. And of course, all of us have heard and read the warnings in airports about carrying packages for someone in our luggage. Yesterday morning, around six a.m., I overheard the Pensione owner and the Bassae Shepherd having an argument in the service yard below my window. They were speaking in Greek, and I couldn't understand of course, but they were terribly angry with each other."

Miss Crawford nodded. "I see. Thank you, Emma, for telling me this. You were right of course to refuse to take the package.

"I shall telephone the Inspector as soon as we reach Athens. I may as well tell you, the Pensione Anastasia owner has been under surveillance by the police for some time. He is suspected of having Greek-Cypriot sympathies. It is quite possible he is a member of a political group trying to raise money for the Greek-Cypriot cause." She sits down amid a babble of excited voices as the students take in what they have just heard.

The coach steadily winds its way toward Athens, over and around barren hills with scant vegetation where the occasional shepherd's hut dots the landscape and few villages line the route. Emma thinks about what Miss Crawford has told them. So the Bassae Shepherd had been right. Her disclosures confirm that there is a stolen treasure, an Amulet of Apollo, buried for centuries and now unearthed, missing from its hiding place.

A frisson of fear grips Emma. Someone may have looked through her bureau drawer after all, but why? Why me? What is my connection? Unless they were seeking someone to be their courier and wanted an American, not a British passport holder. That must be it. She fears the Bassae Shepherd may be fighting alone in this one-sided battle, a battle to preserve an important artifact for his country. But perhaps Maria Crawford and the police will prove to be a powerful ally for him.

However, neither Emma nor anyone on the coach knows that inside the Pensione Anastasia, before the bags were loaded, one of those bags, a case from Emma and Jane's room, received a special mark, a tiny Doric column sketched in chalk, marking the bag for unknown eyes when it reaches its final destination, Heathrow airport.

~

A plethora of riches awaits them at the Acropolis Museum in Athens. Gee, unable to make the arduous climb to the entrance, passes the time comfortably at a sidewalk cafe facing the ancient and beautiful Temple of the Winds, where the coach sets down. Fiona, who has visited the museum several times earlier, stays with her to keep her company.

In the Acropolis Museum as the students read the printed cards in the blank wall spaces where missing sculptures would have been displayed, they feel embarrassed. A silence falls on the group as they read, "Pediment sculptures from the Parthenon taken without permission and placed in the British Museum, London."

"How perfectly horrible," says Rosamund. "It makes me ashamed I'm British." Some of the others murmur in agreement.

But Emma, taking the role as the impartial American, quickly speaks up, "But who is to say Lord Elgin didn't really do the Greeks a great service? Had he not cared enough about the pediment sculptures, and whatever else he shipped off, they might have been plundered and used as building materials, or blown up in wars with the Turks. I remember reading that a bomb was set off in the Parthenon in one of those battles. At least he saved some of the figures. And also, I've read that his letters state he did obtain official permission from the Greek authorities to remove the sculptures."

"And now they want them back," murmurs Sam at her elbow.

"And back they'll go in my opinion," adds Miss Crawford, who overhears Sam's remark, "though perhaps not in our lifetime. Public opinion in the world is very important, and we live in an age celebrating nationalism, not colonialism. Over all the world, many people believe we should give them back. But lest we leave thinking all is lost, I want to point out the beautiful Peplos Kore here." Students cluster around her.

"She was one of a number of decorative ornaments on the Acropolis, but note the humanization of the figure, the exquisitely realized facial features, the traces of remaining color. Too often we forget the ancient world's architecture and sculpture were alive with color!

"And the date makes it even more astounding, five hundred thirty BC!"

Temple of the Winds, Athens

The Parthenon, Acropolis, Athens

Parthenon Sculpture, Lapith and Centaur,
Elgin Marbles, British Museum

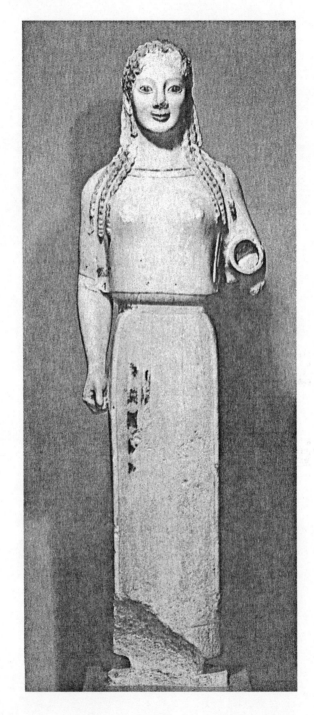

Peplos Kore, Acropolis Museum, Athens

Jockey, 2nd C. B.C., National Museum, Athens

Detail: Bronze figure: From the Artemisium Wreck.
Figure over life size.
National Museum, Athens.

The Erechtheum with Caryatids, Acropolis, Athens

The coach picks up Gee and Fiona and the students, then travels to a second museum, the National Museum in the heart of Athens. Once inside, they marvel as treasure after treasure comes into view: the towering bronze figure a man holding a thunderbolt, a sculpture brought up from the sea; the marble figure of a youth holding a fillet of about four hundred forty BC shows the classical style at its perfection. There is a remarkable figure of a boy jockey, so lifelike as he urges on his horse, he seems bursting with verve and animation.

Miss Crawford tells them the horse and jockey were unearthed many miles apart, and at last are reunited in the museum. After touring the galleries, Emma's admiration for early Greek sculptors grows. And their influence on subsequent art is impossible to calculate, she realizes.

Footsore and weary, the group leaves the museum in late afternoon. "I think we have just enough time for a last Greek coffee in Constitution Square before going to the airport," says Miss Crawford.

Bounded by tree-lined avenues, Constitution Square dominates the busy heart of Athens. Emma and Sam, choose one of the small tables at a sidewalk café, one of many surrounding the square. Sipping small coffees, they watch traffic hurtling by as they savor the end of their Greek idyll. Seated behind a low hedge with a canopy of tree branches overhead, they enjoy a secluded point from which to view the bustling scene and at the same time recap their experiences of the past two weeks.

"It won't be the same in London," Emma muses somewhat regretfully.

"No, but in some ways it will be good to get back. You'll be meeting the students again at the Gower Street Cafe in two weeks. You can compare notes on the trip from a distance then. It should be a good thing to give your impressions time to settle, don't you think?"

"But remember, I won't be seeing you in classes," Emma adds, nodding. "You'll be slaving away at Guy's Hospital, working the midnight shift, if that sadistic registrar is really as bad as you paint him," she smiles, determined to keep the tone light.

"He's just trying to make a good doctor out of me," Sam smiles ruefully. "He didn't really think I should come on this trip, you know. He wanted me to stay in England and write a paper. Actually, he suggested I hop up to Cambridge and work for a couple of weeks in the Christopher Wren library there. His idea of an inspiring holiday."

"What a bizarre man," Emma says. "So what is this paper you're meant to be writing? Is it about setting broken bones?"

But before Sam can launch into an explanation, an eerie screeching of brakes destroys the ordinary hum of traffic and the peace of the square as a small, blue car, seemingly careening out of control, crosses over two lanes, spins crazily toward the curb, hitting a lone pedestrian in the crosswalk. The car then changes course abruptly and speeds off without stopping. Cries of outrage from people on all sides ring out as those nearest to the victim hurry to him.

Sam, on his feet in a second, makes for the figure lying on the crosswalk. "I am a doctor, let me through, please," he speaks quietly but firmly, edging his way forward. Sensing his mission, the crowd parts to let him pass.

Emma hurries behind him as fast as she can. She sees Sam raise the man's head and cradle it in his arms. The man's eyes are open. Sam bends closer, listening. Then Emma sees the head fall back, the eyes close. Sam tries to find a pulse, a heartbeat. Feverishly he begins trying to resuscitate the man. Finally Sam raises sad eyes to a policeman kneeling beside him.

"He's gone, I'm afraid."

The dead man is wearing a neat shirt and dark trousers. Clean-shaven, carrying a cheap briefcase, his face calm in death, Emma finds him compelling, and vaguely familiar. Quickly she looks at Sam in alarm. Almost imperceptibly he nods to her.

Emma's eyes widen. The dead man is the Bassae Shepherd, but in a much altered state. He has visited a barber, shaved off his beard, and has acquired new clothes and a briefcase. In fact, he now looks as unremarkable as one of the hundreds of office workers walking the busy streets of Athens. And at this moment he is lying dead on the pavement in the middle of the afternoon rush hour.

Sam makes his report to the police officer who arrives promptly on the scene along with a screaming police ambulance which carries the body away. A somewhat grey-faced Miss Crawford verifies Sam's statement about the man to the authorities, stating that she and members of her group have encountered him on several occasions in recent days.

It is apparent she is greatly disturbed, and has concerns for the safety of her students. She wants to get them aboard their plane safely bound for Heathrow as soon as possible. The police official takes names and addresses of Sam and Miss Crawford, giving permission for the group to depart.

Emma, usually calm and in control, has a bad case of nerves. She has this minute overheard Sam telling the policeman that the man's last words were "going to Heathrow," just before he died in Sam's arms. What could that mean?

~

It is an edgy, exhausted, strangely silent group of students who climb gratefully aboard the British Airways jet at Athens airport. They appear drained and still in shock, having witnessed a hit and run death which amazingly turns out to be someone they know. Almost the minute the plane is airborne some of them drop off in a fitful slumber while others feign sleep, wishing to be alone. There is little whispering or idle chatter. Those who cannot sleep sit silently buckled in with their own thoughts.

But was it an accident? Emma wonders as, sleepless, she turns the events of their last hours in Athens over in her mind. She is almost certain that not all of the students are aware of the identity of the victim. Some of them had been taking their coffee a great distance away from the accident. Only Sam, Miss Crawford and a few others got a close look at the figure lying on the street, and he looked completely different in his new clothes and neatly cut hair. Had the police advised him? Or had fear for his safety driven him to take simple precautions on his own? Emma wishes she could be sitting nearer to Sam, to hear his thoughts on what has happened. But he is seated several rows back, eyes closed, giving every appearance of sleeping.

Emma realizes the shepherd must have made his way to Athens and sought help from the police. The police knew enough from what Miss Crawford had told them to make them listen with interest to everything the shepherd had to say. But, she reasons, the police also must have realized the danger was real; they must be the ones who provided him with the disguise, told him to shave off his beard, restyle his hair, carry a briefcase. But it was not enough. Whoever had been driving that car was looking for the shepherd with lethal intent, and what is more, accomplished their deadly mission. It was murder.

Emma understands the stakes in this puzzle of the missing Apollo Amulet have risen sharply. The thieves will stop at nothing, not even murder, to gain their own ends. Emma feels a spasm of fear ripple through her body. What will be their next move? In a couple of hours the safety capsule of the flying plane will no longer exist. They will set down at Heathrow, where dark, unseen forces will be free to do their work. She looks at Jane, sleeping fitfully beside her. Did Jane realize who the victim was? Emma thinks she did not. Perhaps none of us will be safe when we land. Who can know what will happen next?

It is an evil, monstrous conspiracy, she thinks angrily, a plan which must not succeed. The forces of good must outweigh the forces of evil. But Emma is uneasy. Her thoughts turn to Sam. He has hardly enjoyed a carefree holiday. First Gee's fall which sent him into action, transporting her to a doctor, standing by while the bone was set and a cast applied. Then running to the aid of the shepherd when he was hit by the car. Trying and failing to resuscitate him. Hearing the dying man's final words 'going to Heathrow' before he expired.

No wonder Sam is apparently asleep. He must be exhausted mentally and physically. Emotionally too. In his demanding work at the hospital, he is adept at snatching a few moments rest when the opportunity presents itself. He must be sleeping, after all. Emma wishes she too could fall into the oblivion of sleep.

Her thoughts jump to the airport in London. Heathrow, that megalith of moving planes, travelers, baggage handlers, flight crews, mechanics, shopkeepers, food suppliers, customs officers, ticket takers, dishwashers, parking attendants, all perambulating like ants along its tunnels and corridors in buses, trains, taxis, underground trains and on foot. What a perfect place for deception and intrigue, for anyone wishing to operate outside the law. Heathrow is like a gargantuan spider web of activity where most people are anonymous. She must be wary, on her guard.

'Going to Heathrow'. What did it mean? Surely, Emma reasons, the dying man was referring to the Apollo Amulet. He certainly wasn't flying to England himself. What else could it be? All his frantic efforts since that afternoon when he suddenly appeared before them at the Temple of Bassae had been focused on the amulet's recovery, preventing the thieves who had stolen it from transporting it abroad. Had he discovered identity of the thieves? Found out they were planning to get the amulet to London, then sell it?

Think, Emma, think! She wills herself, eyes closed, as the plane draws nearer and nearer to London with every passing minute. If you were the thieves, what would you do? The answer has to be to get the amulet on a plane bound for Heathrow, then intercept it when it arrives. But the task seems impossible, so many flights every day from Athens to London. How could anyone, even the police, hope to find out on which flight it is coming in, let alone how it is arriving? In a suitcase, a rucksack, in the freight bay? Again the thought presents itself to her: An amulet is something very tiny to hide, not large, like a painting, or a statue. Athens police had gone to the trouble to have the group's baggage secured, to prevent anyone from inserting an object into their cases, but had they done it soon enough? And did they have information they weren't revealing? Emma wonders.

At last she drops off in a light, uneasy sleep only to be awakened in minutes by the flight attendant's announcement that landing preparations are underway.

Emma and Jane join the students walking along the rabbit-warren corridors leading to the immigration area. Jane and the others wait in the European Community line while Emma with her American passport stands in the line of "All Other Passports." Sam mouths to her, "See you at the baggage claim."

Emma's queue crawls at a snail's pace. Jane and the others will be in central London before I get through this line, she thinks glumly as she waits. But surprisingly, she gets through quickly after all. Others ahead of her, large families immigrating to the United Kingdom from places like India, Pakistan, Jamaica, Bangladesh, are moved to another line. The pale young man at the customs desk summons her forward.

He wants to know the nature of her trip to Greece. Looking at her visa in the back of the passport, he reminds her that she is admitted to the UK for one year of study only. He smiles, stamps the entry seal on her passport, and waves her on.

Reunited at the baggage claim with the others, Emma says goodbye as members of the group claim their cases and begin to drift away. She observes Miss Crawford pointing out her case to Lance who in turn signals a porter to load it onto his trolley. Gee sits calmly in a wheelchair with Fiona standing by, waiting for the chauffeured car sent by the university to take them to their homes.

Emma and Jane decide to take the tube to Knightsbridge. From the underground station they can hail a taxi first to Jane's house in Montpelier Square, then on to Chesham Place to the Belfrage flat. The Belfrages are away on holiday in France, and Emma dreads going home to an empty flat at midnight. But first they must wait until Jane's case shows up on the carousel. Her train of thought is interrupted by Sam who has collected his case, and is preparing to leave.

"Emma, when will I see you?" he calls to her, case in hand, raincoat slung over his shoulder.

"Whenever you can get away from Guy's and those broken bones," she counters lightly, knowing he has her telephone number.

She is determined to avoid heavy farewells. She realizes this rapport, this admiration they have for each other may evaporate, now that the trip is over. Probably just a summer fling, she thinks. Sam surely views it as a pleasant interlude, nothing more. Thoughtfully Emma acknowledges this possibility as she looks at Sam's disappearing figure going down moving stairs toward the underground.

"Thursday evening?" He calls back to her. She nods. "I'll ring you," he says, giving her a brief wave before vanishing out of sight.

He isn't one who enjoys displays of affection in public. And I admire him all the better for it. I like restraint. I've seen too much of an all-out, 'go for it' culture and I don't like it. Slow and steady is my goal. I don't wish to be one of the hares. Tortoises suit me just fine. Emma collects her thoughts and her belongings, smiles to herself, content.

"You must be in a trance, Emma," Jane tugs at her sleeve. "Your case is circling around the carousel. Grab it, and as soon as mine comes up, we'll be off."

Emma removes her bag from the carousel; they wait, but Jane's luggage fails to appear. The carousel shudders to a stop. The few unclaimed bags are lifted off and placed in a heap to one side, but Jane's case is not among them. The entire group of students has vanished; and more travelers are crowding around as the arrival of another flight is announced. Jane and Emma head to the baggage claim office. The Indian superintendent in charge tries his best to make Jane feel better.

"You are not to be worrying, Mees," he intones in a sing song voice, friendly dark eyes smiling at her. "This is happening to peoples occasionally. Your case will come in on a later flight, I'm being certain of it. And we will deliver it to you personally at your home in Montpelier Square tomorrow." He smiles a sweet smile with the greatest sincerity, showing large white teeth.

Cheered somewhat by his confidence, a dispirited Jane carries their raincoats and Emma lugs her case toward the tube. They buy tickets to Knightsbridge station and run to catch a train whose doors are about to glide shut.

"Bet you ten pence it's raining when we get off at Knightsbridge," Emma sighs with a grin as they collapse into their seats.

"Oh Emma, I'm so glad to be back in England, I don't care. This turned out to be such a frightful day, and now my case has gone missing. I'm so worried about all that has happened."

"Jane Hale, you are hopeless. We've been on a marvelous two week sojourn in sunny Greece and you're glad to be back in the permanent mists of England. There is simply no accounting for taste." Her face became serious and she adds, "not that I'm indifferent about the hit and run death of the poor man earlier today. That was horrible. But you mustn't worry, and Jane, I'm certain they'll find your case. Probably just a simple mix-up at the airport in Athens, like the man said."

Time to reveal the dead man's identity later, after Jane has had a good night's rest. But Emma feels odd, not telling Jane who the man was. I just don't think she can handle any more tonight, Emma decides, and they fall silent as the tube rumbles through the night. At Knightsbridge they come up from the Underground on the moving staircase into a light rain.

"Here's your ten pence, Emma," Jane says, laughing as they go directly to the taxi queue in front of the beautiful old Hyde Park Hotel, its windows agleam with lights and a uniformed doorman standing by who greets them cordially and blows his whistle for a taxi. Looking back at the flowering window boxes of the hotel bathed in creamy light of street lamps softened by the mist, Emma reflects that it is indeed good to be back in wonderful, familiar London, rain or not. But she is fearful, as she reviews the hours of their harrowing departure from Athens. Then, the disappearance of Jane's bag. What unseen forces are at work?

When the taxi rolls up to Jane's house in Montpelier Square they see that here, too, lights gleam from all the windows.

"Good grief, Mummy must be having one of her evenings. With a little luck I can slink up unnoticed." Quickly Jane gathers up raincoat and purse.

Emma knows Jane hates these parties. People she does not know, with interests she does not share. Being introduced by her glamorous mother, as 'my little bookworm, Jane'. Emma gives Jane a quick peck on the cheek and promises to ring her in the morning.

The taxi eases away, leaving Knightsbridge, traveling toward the quiet, tree-lined streets of nearby Belgravia. At Emma's flat on Chesham Place, the porter's desk is still lighted, Emma notes with relief, and Hawkins springs to the door taking her case from the taxi driver before she has time to gather up her remaining belongings.

"Oh, Hawkins, I'm so glad you're still at your desk. It's been such a long, trying day and I'm simply exhausted." She follows the tall, slightly stooped porter, marching along proudly in his uniform, as they enter into the lift and she fumbles through her purse for keys to the flat.

Alighting at the fourth floor, Hawkins unlocks the big mahogany door to the flat with its beautiful panels of Victorian stained glass and begins turning on lights. The warmth, the comfort of the rooms seem especially welcoming to Emma as she glances at the pretty, pale watercolours lining the walls, the well-worn patina of mellow wood furniture, soft grey draperies of a heavily patterned damask. She notes the faint smell of lavender polish. Everything is orderly, safe looking.

Hawkins, sets down her bag, looks carefully about. His calm voice reassures Emma. "Everything seems all right, Miss Hale. Would you like me to check the rest of the flat?"

"Yes, please, Hawkins, if you could. I'd be so grateful." He returns after looking into the rooms along both hallways and pronounces everything in order. "I've left your hallway and bedroom lighted, Miss Hale. Will that be all?"

"That's all, Hawkins. And thank you so much. Oh, could you have the milk man leave me two pints of milk, and of course I'd like The Telegraph."

It has been over two weeks that she has not read the English papers. She relishes the newspapers in England with great attention to detail, and the small stories of bizarre and unusual happenings sandwiched in between major news of the day. Being home is good.

FOUR

Scotland Yard on the Case

The following morning Emma finishes unpacking and makes her way to the kitchen for a bowl of Wheet-a-Bix, her favourite wheat cereal. Sitting in the light-filled kitchen, cheerful with Laura Ashley wallpaper of a sunny yellow background with tiny white flowers and a matching valance, she reads The Telegraph. Wide windows overlook the inner courtyard from five floors up.

Frances Belfrage has indulged her love of growing things in the light-filled kitchen. Pots of ivy, philodendron and Busy Lizzie flourish, tumbling over the top of a big Welsh dresser filled with yellow pottery. A copper bowl at the center of the scrubbed pine table holds more ivy. Sunlight, fleeting and obscured at moments by scudding clouds, shines peevishly. A typical London morning, Emma thinks. It is good to be home again. The double ring of the telephone interrupts her thoughts as she pours a second cup of coffee.

"Emma. Jane here. They delivered my case about thirty minutes ago, and guess what? They found it last night, not incoming on another flight, but in a lavatory at Heathrow! It had been opened and messed about and abandoned. The name tags were torn off, but Mr. Patel, that nice man at the baggage claim, matched it to my description. Can you credit it?" Jane's voice is one of disbelief.

"Is there anything missing?" Emma asks quickly.

"No, nothing. That's what is so strange. Even Granny's pearls are there. If they went to the trouble of nicking the case, why, what were they after? Mummy and I can't figure."

What indeed, thinks Emma, her thoughts flying to the Apollo Amulet. But she shouldn't alarm Jane yet. "And you are reasonably sure all your belongings are intact?"

"I think so," Jane replies. "I found a packing list I'd made on my dresser before we left for Greece, and it all checks. But Emma, there's something funny about my case. On the outside there's a strange chalk mark, a tiny sketch of a column fragment." A lengthy pause follows.

"Emma!" Jane screeches suddenly, "You don't think they put the amulet in my suitcase?"

The very real possibility fills Emma with alarm. It certainly seems that Jane has hit on the truth, but she is careful to keep her voice calm.

"Now, Jane, steady on. Let's just take this slowly and not jump to conclusions."

The mark was put on in Greece, of course, Emma's racing thoughts silently confirm. At the Pensione Anastasia. Unnoticed in the rush and bustle of departure, it had been a sign to the person whose job it was to steal the bag, and extract the amulet. There seems to be no getting around it. Best tell Jane in person, not over the phone, she reasons. Yes, definitely break this unwelcome news in person.

"Jane, what do you say we meet for a bite of lunch at the Serpentine restaurant in Hyde Park about one o'clock? We can go over everything face to face and get to the bottom of this," Emma proposes, glancing at her watch.

"Splendid. Mummy was hinting at the breakfast table about shopping this afternoon and this will get me off the hook. She'll be pleased I'm meeting you. Thanks Emma. See you at one at the Serpentine restaurant."

"Jane," Emma adds, reconsidering her plan. "Go through everything in your suitcase before we meet. Be sure there's nothing hidden, in a side pocket, for example. Something small, the size of an amulet, I mean. Because of the mark on your case, it may have been designated as the carrier. That must be why they stole it."

"Surely not. But I'll get busy. Wouldn't that be a stunner, finding the missing amulet?"

Slowly Emma puts down the telephone, her mind racing furiously. Someone at the Pensione Anastasia put a mark on Jane's case, alerting the London accomplice to intercept it before Jane plucked it off the carousel.

That unknown person quickly made off with Jane's case and took it to a lavatory where he forced it open, looking for something hidden inside, the amulet, presumably.

The point is, did he find it? And how did it get there? Funny, they ask me to take the package, then mark Jane's bag. Does that mean the amulet was put by mistake inside my bag? Or did they mark Jane's by mistake?

She leaves the kitchen and goes to her bedroom, takes her case down from the top of the wardrobe. No mark of any kind on it. She opens the case and looks inside. Nothing. Completely empty. She opens bureau drawers looking at underclothes and blouses neatly transferred from her case.

She examines the clothes hanging in the wardrobe. No tell-tell bulges in pockets, nothing smallish stuffed into hems. Nothing.

Satisfied at last, Emma showers. Oh the bliss of a steady stream of warm water, after the erratic plumbing of Greece. She dresses in a kilt skirt of a Scottish clan plaid and white blouse and leaves the flat for her meeting with Jane.

Hawkins is nowhere to be seen as she lets herself out the latched doors into the street. Probably having his elevenses. Nothing, but nothing interrupts Hawkins' tea time. Plane trees line the sidewalks, making Belgravia seem more like a village than part of one of the world's greatest cities. She walks several blocks into Sloane Street, past the Carleton Tower Hotel and up to the top where Harvey Nichols store and the Hyde Park Hotel, symbols of the heart of Knightsbridge, stand. As she walks past the hotel, she waves to the distinguished doorman who remembers her from last night, smiles, and tips his top hat.

Turning deeper into Knightsbridge she passes the Underground entrance, where flower and newspaper vendors man their stalls. Reaching the big department store Harrods, she crosses over Knightsbridge, goes down Knightsbridge Alley, next into Knightsbridge Green. There she sees the Horse Guards' barracks, where the Queen stables her horses behind high brick walls. The horses are out of sight, but she can hear their neighing and catch the faint whiff of the stable yard. Horses living in the heart of London, horses taking their pre-dawn canter daily down the wide streets of Knightsbridge, Chelsea and Belgravia! On mornings when she awakes early, she often hears the clacking of their hooves down Chesham Place. Oh, the bliss of living here, in this magical place.

She enters the cool, green bower of Hyde Park where mothers gossip on benches while children play on a newly installed jungle gym. Horseback riders, wearing tight jodhpurs and black velvet riding hats, gallop on the sand track encircling the enormous park. Commodious prams pushed by nannies in uniform expose their tiny charges to the fresh morning air. Couples aimlessly strolling, elderly couples chatting on benches, poorly-dressed students reading paperback novels or volumes of poetry as they stride past businessmen wearing bowler hats, smartly stepping along gravel paths crossing the park. Oh the richness of it!

Emma watches as two flower children with spiky orange and pink hair glide weightlessly along on roller skates, carefully finessing their way past shuffling old ladies with shopping baskets. For all their fierce makeup and embellishments, the boy and girl appear young and strangely vulnerable. They blow friendly kisses to strangers they meet along the path. Emma views them like innocents, children in their daunting hairstyles.

Jane is waiting for her inside the restaurant whose glass window walls overlook the peaceful waters of the Serpentine. Rowboats drift on the mirror of the lake and flotillas of ducks paddle close to the banks, hoping for toss-outs from a national population of unabashed bird and animal lovers.

"Isn't it great to be home?" Jane exclaims, greeting Emma with a hug and beaming happily. She really is extraordinarily pretty. Emma studies the sparkling grey eyes and blooming skin. And she has no idea how lovely she is, that is what's so wonderful.

"Travel is broadening, Jane," Emma twigs her gently. "How can you know home is best if you never see the rest of the world?"

"I do realize travel is important, Emma," answers Jane seriously as she studies the menu.

Quickly she turns to Emma "I'll confide in you, Emma. Last night, I dreamed of Sounion and the temple of Poseidon. I didn't dream about the amulet at all! I kept seeing those cliffs all around with the deep blue of the sea below the temple ruins, and I thought I would give anything to be back in Greece again! No wonder Lord Byron loved that spot so much!" She smiles, turning back to the menu.

They order egg and chips for Jane and a cheese and chutney salad for Emma. "Now, what are we going to do about this mystery?" Jane asks, sipping orange squash.

Emma sits up straight and begins to summarize. "Well, a famous amulet, a treasure from ancient Greece, has disappeared. The police think that someone tried to get it out of the country to sell either here or in America."

Emma pauses to reflect, then continues. "The police are suspicious of the staff at the Pensione Anastasia where we stayed. Does that mean our group is pulled into the mystery?" Leaving the question unanswered she goes on, "A man was killed in Athens yesterday, a man loudly proclaiming theft of the treasure, an ancient amulet put into his hands for safekeeping."

"You mean that hit and run accident?" Jane breaks in, her eyes wide. Somehow, as Emma guessed, in all the excitement she failed to realize who the victim was.

"Surely that man was not the Bassae Shepherd? He dressed differently. His hair was trimmed and he had no beard."

"But it was the Bassae Shepherd," Emma answers her calmly. "He was cleaned up and carrying a briefcase because he wanted to be disguised. He was afraid. It's not likely his death was an accident, Jane. Somebody wanted him out of the way permanently, it would seem. Then, there is also the mystery of your missing case."

Jane is struggling to come to grips with this startling new information. "Emma, if the thieves wanted to, they could have slipped the amulet in anyone's bag before we ever left Olympia. While we were still at the Pensione Anastasia."

"But the person on this end had to know what to look for in a bag or case. A bag to be checked was the perfect choice. Unattended on the carousel for a minute, it could be spirited quickly away, to the safe haven of a lavatory," Emma thoughtfully rubs her chin.

Temple of Poseidon, Sounion

"And goodness knows our cases were lying about unlocked in the Pensione Anastasia for hours on end before we boarded the coach. Remember how we packed at several different times, when we could snatch a few minutes? Someone put the amulet in the wrong case, perhaps, or even more likely, the person who marked your case made a mistake and should have put the mark on mine. Remember, Lydia asked me to carry that package. But I've searched my case and everything in it and can find nothing! It is so frustrating, Jane!"

"I think the time has come for you to call Miss Crawford," Jane declares.

But when they find a call box outside the restaurant and dial the number of the University of London Extra-Mural offices, they are told Miss Crawford is not in and will not return to her desk until the following Monday morning. Nothing Emma can say will persuade the office secretary to give Emma her teacher's personal telephone number. She is told very politely that it is strictly against university regulations.

"Emma," Jane says as she puts down the telephone, "This is serious. If we can't reach Miss Crawford, we'd better notify Scotland Yard."

"All right. I agree," said Emma. "I just wish I could figure it out. I feel like I'm circling round and round the truth, and just missing it. I wish Sam were here. Jane, what do you think the Bassae Shepherd's last words were?" Jane shakes her head.

"They were 'going to Heathrow'. Sam heard him say it as he held him, just before he died." Emma swallows. "But what did he mean? Well, I'll ring Scotland Yard now."

When she reports to Scotland Yard from the call box with Jane standing by, the impersonal, polite voice of the dispatcher displays a minimum of interest.

"Someone will either telephone you or come to interview you within twenty four hours, Miss. All right?"

Thanking him politely, Emma replaces the receiver. Apparently she and Jane have done everything they can at the moment. It is time to be patient and wait.

The two part company at the edge of Hyde Park. Jane hurries to meet her mother at Harrods for a shopping expedition. Emma hurries to do some shopping at the greengrocer. Absentmindedly she looks over the fresh fruits and vegetables, selecting a lettuce, some apples and oranges. Next she purchases a packet of sausage rolls and a Dundee cake from Sainsburys on the opposite side of the street. She knows the pantry in the flat is amply stocked with tins of soup and other staples, it is fresh food she needs.

Hawkins the porter is at his post in the vestibule. He hurries to hold wide the door as she enters, displaying the well-oiled efficiency of an army veteran. Emma wonders what branch of the military he served. He certainly has the mannerisms of a military man. The residents of the building can depend on him to keep a close watch on the happenings of Thirty-Four Chesham Place.

As she unlocks the door to her flat she hears the double ring of the telephone. Setting down her shopping bag, she hurries to answer, but when she speaks, no one replies and in a few seconds the line goes dead. Now who could that have been, she thinks with a slight twinge of unease.

Later, after her solitary dinner, she switches on the radio to listen to the long-running daily saga of the Archers. Radio sets all over England are tuned in to the Archers at this early time of evening. Very little seems to happen, but the long-running drama has worked its way into the national consciousness. Even the Queen Mother is an avid fan, Emma has heard.

Restless, she picks up the Daily Telegraph once more. Nothing there about the missing amulet, however. Not that she really expected it. When Scotland Yard appears to be indifferent, reporters certainly won't be concerned. Bored, she listens through the lengthy, nightly shipping report on the wireless, marveling that such a small island can experience every sort of weather from coast to coast in the space of twenty four hours. When the wireless program "A Book at Bedtime" begins, she loses herself in the story and relaxes, managing to prepare for bed with peaceful thoughts.

~

Mrs. Mudge, the cleaning lady, commences ringing the bell at the front door of the flat by nine-thirty. Guiltily Emma slips on her robe and runs to let her inside. She has overslept, and Wednesday, she tardily remembers, is cleaning day.

Unfailingly cheerful and hard working, the tiny and wiry Mrs. Mudge possesses a stubborn will and the stamina needed to wield the mops and brooms. Her dark coat and hat, the latter sporting a bedraggled rose, have seen better days, but Mrs. Mudge's spirit is not wilted. Thinning grey hair twisted into a bun at the back of her neck, she never removes her hat. In fact, Emma reflects, I've never seen her without it.

Mrs. Mudge is smiling good-naturedly when Emma lets her in, despite poor, crooked teeth which have bitten into too many chocks and peppermints. Emma guesses those teeth would challenge the most stout-hearted orthodontist, should he ever come face to face with Mrs. Mudge in his chair.

"So, yers back! Stock up at the duty-free did yer?"

It amazes Emma how many package tour travelers in England seem to take more interest in the duty-free shopping than in their experiences in Barcelona or the Canary Islands or Marbella.

"Yes, I'm back, and I brought a carton of Silk Cut cigarettes just for you, Mrs. Mudge." Emma smiles, handing over the parcel.

Mrs. Mudge's lined face lights up with pleasure. "Yer never! Well that's very kind of yer, I'm sure," she adds graciously. "My 'Enry will thank yer fer these."

Emma dresses hurriedly so she can join Mrs. Mudge at the kitchen table for the ritual cup of tea before she begins her cleaning duties. This is the time for Mrs. Mudge to bring Emma into the picture about her Henry's lumbago, how her son Marvin and his wife Maureen plan going on a package to Malaga in a couple of weeks.

Then, remembering Emma has just returned from foreign shores herself, she inquires politely, "Was the water fit to drink?" Emma replies that indeed it was, just as the doorbell sounds.

Two immaculately groomed, card-carrying Scotland Yard detectives stand waiting. Emma ushers them into the drawing room and firmly closes the double doors, catching a glimpse of Mrs. Mudge peering from the hallway, a-quiver with curiosity.

Scotland Yard looks impressive, Emma has to admit. Inspector Harper, the older of the two and Inspector St. Cyr, not only project the image of glamorous detectives, they appear to be extremely intelligent. By the time they stop questioning her, Emma feels they have extracted every drop of information to be gleaned. She gives them the names of Miss Crawford, Sam, and Jane. At the close of the interview they thank her, rising to leave.

"Inspector St. Cyr will be handling this case," the one called Harper reveals. "Please report any further information you might have to him, Miss Darling."

Charles St. Cyr presses a small card into her hands. Tall, brown-haired and very handsome, he is the younger, more relaxed of the two, completely at home in his impeccably tailored suit.

"And what did you think of the Temple of Bassae?" he asks unexpectedly, a smile hovering on his lips as they move toward the door.

"Without a doubt, it is the most remarkable temple and setting we saw," Emma replies. "Have you been there?" He nods.

"Several years back, with a history group when I was a student. Being up among those spectacular ruins was the highlight of my trip. There is an aura about Bassae unlike any place I've ever seen. I'll never forget it." The smile fades and he is suddenly focused on business again.

"Don't hesitate to ring me at this number anytime, day or night, Miss Darling." As she closes the door she glances at the card again. Charles St. Cyr. Strange name for a policeman. She wonders if the pair will pay Jane a call.

~

Later that morning Jane rings to tell Emma the detectives from the Yard have just left Montpelier Square, taking her suitcase with them. "They wanted to inspect it more closely," Jane says. "They wouldn't say a word about what they thought, whether it might have carried the amulet or not."

"Scotland Yard never gives out any information. They collect it." Emma says. "At least, that's the way it happens in books and the films. So we really don't know anything more, now that they've visited us. Frustrating they didn't reveal even the tiniest thing they were thinking."

"Maybe," Jane admits. "But I feel safer. Did they leave you a card? I think Mr. St. Cyr is awfully good looking, don't you?"

Mrs. Mudge is manning the hoover, clattering away in the dining room, when the two rings of the telephone sound through the flat. For the second time Emma answers, the telephone line goes dead. This is crazy. Who can be calling and hanging up?

She and Mrs. Mudge share a sausage roll and soup lunch. Around three, Mrs. Mudge, having polished and shined every visible surface in the flat to glowing perfection, prepares to leave, proudly clutching the airport shopping bag containing the Silk Cuts.

"Cheers, Luv! See yer next week!"

Emma decides to shampoo any lingering dust of Greece out of her hair. As she climbs out of the shower, hair dripping, the street buzzer sounds. Quickly she reaches for her robe, wraps her hair quickly in a towel, and goes to the inter-phone.

"Yes?" she inquires, lifting the receiver. The only sound is the hum of traffic from below. What can be going on? She replaces the receiver firmly and presses the buzzer for Hawkins. He appears at the door promptly, barely time for Emma to slip into her clothes.

"Hawkins, someone has been ringing my street buzzer. I wonder if you've seen anyone strange looking or suspicious at the door?"

"I'll go down and have a look, Miss Darling. Don't open your door to anyone until I come back."

Emma's heart beats a like a voodoo drum as she stations herself by the front door of the flat. If anyone's trying to rattle me with all this ringing business, they're succeeding. Hawkins reappears to report he can find no one lurking outside, but promises to keep an eye out. Again he cautions Emma about opening her door. Emma, recalling the times she has inwardly scoffed at Hawkins stuffy precautions, does not scoff any longer. She is grateful to him and thanks him warmly. The telephone rings again and she jumps, hurries to answer. It's Sam. Her spirits rise.

"I'm still here at Guy's, but I had an hour off to cat nap and I wanted to hear your voice."

Hearing him, Emma feels reassured and reports to him about the theft of Jane's case and the visit from Scotland Yard. Finally she tells him about the telephone calls when nobody speaks up and the ringing of the street buzzer of the flat when nobody answers. Sam is silent for a long minute.

"Emma, this is worrying. Especially since you are alone in the flat. You have my number here. Ring me if you need to. They can find me quickly. And by all means, since the Scotland Yard inspector gave you his card, call him if anything else suspicious happens. Don't worry. Just keep alert and keep your door locked. Maybe you should think about staying at Jane's tonight. I'm sure she'd be glad to put you up. Then you won't be rattling around in the flat alone."

"Well, I hate to admit defeat, but I think you're right. I'll ring Jane."

"Can I see you tomorrow night?"

"Of course, that is, if you aren't exhausted from your work. You do need time off for a change of scene occasionally," she jokes. "Seriously, Sam, we need to talk more about the amulet; where on earth can it be?"

"I don't know, but I'll expound on any theories I come up with tomorrow night. Be ready at seven? We'll go someplace special for dinner."

Talking to Sam makes Emma forget her anxieties. Thoughtfully she twists a strand of sandy hair which has escaped from the towel. She rings Jane and arranges to spend the night at Montpelier Square. Jane's mother it seems is having another of her evenings and Jane welcomes an opportunity to miss it gracefully.

"Are you sure it won't upset your mother if I turn up?"

"Upset? She'll be thrilled to have me off her hands. We can take plates of the party nosh up to my room and gab away to our heart's content. Bring your notes on Greece, Emma. We can compare notes for the final exam, that is, if we tire of talking about the amulet!"

Dear Jane, she will be a wonderful lecturer. She can give Maria Crawford a run for her money in a few years. Emma deals with her towel-draped hair which by this time is almost dry. She folds pajamas and a few underclothes into her rucksack, changes into a fresh India cotton skirt patterned in prancing tigers and billowing blue waves and a simple white blouse. Five o'clock and time to go.

As she walks into the hallway she notices a letter lying beneath the slot at the front door. But the mail came earlier this morning. Puzzled, she picks it up and opens it.

Flimsy and cheap, the envelope shows no address on the outside. It is unsealed. Quickly with shaking hands and a wildly beating heart, she unfolds a sheet of lined paper.

"We know you are hiding it. You are being watched every minute. If you know what is good for you, give it up. Then you won't get hurt. Don't tell anyone about this note." It is not signed.

Emma grits her teeth to keep them from chattering. She wills her heart to calm down. It's only a note, but she is frightened. *I can't disturb Sam at his work, no matter what he says. I'll have to ring Scotland Yard.*

Charles St. Cyr answers his own telephone, she notes approvingly. "St. Cyr here."

Her pulse racing, Emma reads him the contents of the note, tells him about the ringing street buzzer, the telephone calls when there is no one on the line.

"They definitely think you've got the amulet and they're trying to frazzle you," he says calmly. "Have you anyone in the flat with you, Miss Darling?"

"No, the Belfrages, the friends I live with, are in France until the end of the month. There is a porter on duty of course. I'm just on my way shortly to Jane Hale's house in Montpelier Square to stay the night."

"Good. Better take a taxi. We'll send someone over to keep an eye on your place. These people are slippery, but I am positive they are rank amateurs. We'll get them. And by the way, could you take the note you received along to Miss Hale's house? I'll come by Montpelier Square when I finish up here and take a look at it."

Somewhat reassured, she waters the plants in the kitchen, stands a moment at the sink looking out at the darkening courtyard below, empty but for several garden chairs and pots of greenery. The sun is making a late afternoon appearance over the rooftops as it often does in summer. It will be a fine evening. Somewhat calmed by performing the simple chore of tending the ivy, she prepares to leave.

She goes down the lift to the foyer and finds Hawkins at his desk. She asks him to call up a taxi, explaining she will stay overnight with Miss Hale on Montpelier Square. Quickly Hawkins goes into the street to hail a cabbie. Emma waits inside until he reappears, the taxi noisily idling at the entrance to the building.

Emma can hear the buzz of conversation and occasional laughter inside as she rings the bell at Montpelier Square. A fluty voice calls, "I'll get it."

It must be Jane's mother, Emma thinks, curious to see her; she appears to be so unlike her daughter.

Felicity Hale is a glitzy copy of her daughter. They could be sisters Emma speculates, but while Jane's beauty is unadorned, fresh and unassuming, her mother's appearance seems sharper, more contrived; she obviously has marshaled all the forces at her disposal to enhance nature. Her nails are carefully varnished light pink, her hair colored ash blonde, helped along by rinses. Her grey eyes are clear like Jane's, but emphasize skillful application of just the right tone of eye shadow and careful plucking of the brows.

Her deceptively unassuming grey gown, a Jean Muir, hangs fluid and flowing in an effortless yet brilliant cut, complimenting those wonderful eyes. Her welcome to Emma is warm and sincere. She's charming, Emma thinks immediately. I like her.

"I really am so pleased that you and Jane have become friends. She needs companionship, she truly does, and with someone who shares her interests. I know her enthusiasms are somewhat different from mine." Felicity Hale has the grace to blush. She's honest into the bargain, Emma notes approvingly.

"Jane is very popular with our classmates, Mrs. Hale," Emma tells her. "You mustn't think she is a loner. She has lots of friends."

"I'm so glad, and relieved. One is always anxious about an only child, isn't one? And of course, her father and I," Her voice trails off. She gives Emma a dazzling smile.

"Jane has just gone upstairs with some food. You two won't go hungry, I promise you." She points to the stairs.

Emma hurries up and finds Jane at the top of the stairs waiting for her, a large platter of tiny cucumber sandwiches in her hands.

"We'll be away from all the noise back here in my room," Jane says after greeting Emma. "Come on, I'll lead the way."

Emma strolls after her, noting the rich oriental carpets scattered artfully about, along with porcelain and antique furniture. Jane's mother obviously has very expensive tastes, Emma thinks, and Jane's father, a well-known solicitor, must possess "plenty of the ready," as Mrs. Mudge might express it, to keep his ex-wife and daughter in such fine style.

"Mummy's compulsive about antiques," Jane murmurs apologetically. She looks nervously right and left as she sees Emma's interested glance at her surroundings. "I personally prefer a lot less clutter. Come in and first show me the note."

Jane's sitting room is lined with fitted bookshelves along one wall. In her bedroom, twin beds, a desk, comfortable chairs are grouped around a low table, with flowered chintz draperies in a summer garden pattern at the windows and matching slipcovers. The space looks colorful and inviting. But before they can settle in, Felicity's rich voice trills up the staircase.

"Jane, another visitor for you. I'm sending Mr. St. Cyr up."

Jane and Emma exchange glances as Charles St. Cyr rapidly mounts the stairs and the girls lead him toward Jane's sitting room.

"I thought I should have a look at your note right away, Miss Darling," he says smiling. "I hope you two don't mind the intrusion." Large brown eyes lock with Jane's then roam around the beautiful room. "I like your space here, Miss Hale, especially the bookshelves."

Jane face registers pleasure as she lowers her eyes and blushes. Just like a Jane Austen heroine, Emma muses. But with Jane it's not an act. She is completely natural, and hasn't a clue how pretty she is.

Silently Emma hands over the note to Charles St. Cyr. He reads it quickly.

"Just a scare note," he says calmly with contempt, refolding it and slipping it into his pocket. "They won't do anything foolish."

"How can you be so sure? A man was killed day before yesterday in Greece," Emma speaks softly.

"Yes, well, come to that, the Greek-Cypriots feel they have cause for a real grievance. To them it's an undeclared war they are fighting. But it's important for you to realize, they wouldn't try something like that here, not in England Not that we're failing to take your note seriously, Miss Darling. For the record, we're taking it very seriously indeed. May I keep it?" he asks politely, having already put it away in his pocket while at the same time eyeing the plates of sandwiches with interest.

Emma certainly hopes he is serious. Perhaps his elegant nonchalance is meant to create a soothing effect. Immediately she is ashamed at the thought. He seems like a genuinely nice person, completely unpretentious, just himself, and not the type to seek effects.

"Please have some food," Jane offers, the dutiful hostess. "There's orange squash. I, I'm afraid there isn't anything else like wine or beer, but I could give you cola or some Schwepps. And I'm sure we could get you wine or sherry from downstairs," Jane finishes uncertainly.

"Orange squash is topping," Charles replies with enthusiasm, taking a plate and heaping it with finger sandwiches. It appears he's going to make himself right at home, Emma thinks, watching him relax. She and Jane fill their plates and Jane pours more orange squash.

Charlie's boarding school, for he insists they use first names, had been quite near Jane's it develops as the evening unfolds. Jane remembers her school as a horrid prison camp where the water was so cold, ice formed a crust on the wash basins. In winter, she tells them, hot water bottles had to be refilled in the middle of the night because the rooms were so frigid.

"It's much colder in the Midlands than London, Emma," Jane explains.

"We always dreamed and schemed to make a midnight raid on you girls down there to see what you were like," Charlie chuckles heartily. "Of course it came to nothing. We could never have gotten away with it."

"It's just as well your plans came to nothing," Jane reminisces. "Our house mother had ears like an elephant; she could hear a pin drop from downstairs."

Charlie, it develops, had nourished his love of art and history when he went on to University, but in the end he settled on a career with Scotland Yard.

"A favourite uncle of mine inspired me to give it a try," he says. "He was a superintendent before he retired. Cracked the Cosley brothers train robbery if you remember," he mumbles, slightly embarrassed. "It was in all the papers."

Jane's eyes widen with excitement. "Yes, I do remember. He was such a hero. I remember now, his name was 'St. Cyr'."

Charlie turns quickly toward Emma, obviously wanting to turn the conversation away from himself. "And where are your parents, Emma? You said you were living with friends in London."

"My parents live in America, near Charlottesville, Virginia, in the foothills of the Blue Ridge mountains. Actually, I've never been to the Midlands where your boarding schools are, but I spent several summers with my grandmother, at Haslemere, in Surrey."

Charlie glances thoughtfully at his empty plate. "Perhaps you shouldn't be alone in that flat, Emma. We could send someone, a young woman officer, to stay with you."

"Surely that's not necessary," Emma answers quickly, feeling reassured by Charlie's jovial, confident presence. "Anyway I can ask Mrs. Mudge, our Cockney cleaning lady, to stay over tomorrow night. She's done that in the past once when I had a horrible case of flu and the Belfrages were away."

"Well, yes, that would be okay. Just so you aren't alone. Though that old boy who is your porter keeps your building tight as the Bank of England, from what I can tell."

"Yes, Hawkins is a very reliable porter. But someone slipped by him today and succeeded in putting the note through the letterbox at my door," Emma reminds Charlie.

"And Hawkins will answer a few questions from me about that," Charlie drawls. "Not too difficult to ask the porter to deliver a note, or to pose as a delivery man with flowers. Not difficult at all, if you put your mind to it, to get inside a secure building."

Charlie remains until the last sandwich is eaten, the orange squash finished. He and Jane are happily recounting school escapades when he finally stands up to leave.

"Jane, thank you for your warm welcome tonight, and the delightful collation. I'll let myself out." And Jane sighs to Emma after he has gone, "Isn't he a peach?"

FIVE

An Amulet Appears

Mrs. Mudge answers the telephone on the third double ring. "Who yer calling? Ow's that? Wait 'til I turn telly down. Can't 'ear a thing." As the background noise subsides Emma asks Mrs. Mudge to come to the flat around three o'clock the following day.

"There's no cleaning to be done. If you would just come and keep me company, and stay the night too, if you could, please." She explains quickly that she feels lonely in the large flat and the Belfrages are still away. Mrs. Mudge could watch telly in the evening, when Emma is planning to go out.

"Of course, Luv. I'm not surprised yer miss Mr. and Mrs. Belfrage. I told the Missus, I did, that Emma's goin' to miss yer two, they bein' gone for so long. 'Course I can come. I'll be there three sharp. Do me feet good to 'ave a rest. Can do Tuesday Emma, but not Wednesday. It's the bingo, you see."

Mrs. Mudge has a heart as big as the Concorde, but fire, flood or any other catastrophe can't keep her away from her weekly bingo game at the Peckham neighborhood center.

"One night will be just fine, Mrs. Mudge," Emma replies, hoping Scotland Yard can get their act together if help is required on subsequent nights. She says goodnight to Mrs. Mudge and puts down the telephone. Turning to Jane, she announces, "It's all fixed up, then. I just need to be home by three tomorrow afternoon."

As Emma and Jane prepare for bed, they discuss plans for the following day and decide to visit the British Museum for another look at the Elgin Marbles, the sculptures from the Parthenon, dubbed by the students Lord Elgin's Folly. The somewhat resentful signs over the empty spaces in the Acropolis Museum piqued their interest in this national treasure trove of sculpture, claimed by two countries.

"Maybe standing in front of the biggest art heist of all time will sharpen our wits so we can solve our mystery of the stolen amulet, "Emma says.

"Well, you know by now, Emma, the British never do anything by halves," Jane replies saucily. Emma throws a pillow at her.

~

Jane fixes a breakfast of porridge, rashers of bacon, eggs, a toast rack full of whole meal toast with rough-cut marmalade and tea.

"By rights you should not be able to get through that door, Jane Hale, eating such a breakfast! Come to think of it, it isn't breakfast, it's an orgy. Is this what your mother eats?" Emma gapes at the feast Jane has set out before her.

"Oh no, Mummy claims lemon tea and a Ryvita biscuit or two is enough for her," Jane shrugs. "But my Dad taught me to make breakfast like this. 'Everyone needs a proper start to the day, Jane,' he always says. Are two eggs enough?" She nods toward two perfect sunny side up eggs looking up at Emma like accusing eyes.

"More than enough," Emma answers with a sigh, taking up her knife and fork and preparing to eat a day's ration of calories in one sitting. How the British manage such early morning banquets is beyond her. She is gamely getting on with it when Felicity Hale appears, fresh in a crisp housecoat from The White House on Regents Street Emma guesses, noting Felicity's neat coiffure and freshly varnished nails.

"What? Already eating? I was going to make breakfast for you lambs!" Felicity's face, minus the usual make-up, shines with cheerfulness. Again Emma feels drawn to her vibrant personality.

"Oh Mummy, you know we'd faint at mid-morning for sure if you gave us your Ryvita and tea. I say, Emma and I are off to the British Museum in just a tick." Emma observes two pairs of grey eyes lock together as Jane waits for her mother's reply.

Felicity's face falls. "But Jane, I thought perhaps the three of us might have a look in the shops. You know, Browns, Harvey Nichols, Harrods," her voice trails off. She is having a hard time understanding her daughter isn't really interested in clothes, Emma realizes, and it hurts. It's as though Jane's rejecting her.

"Come and go along with us, Mrs. Hale," Emma offers. "We're going to look at the Elgin marbles in the British Museum."

"Oh yes, Pet, I know. One was dragged to see them often enough when one was in school. But I really can't manage it today. I have to be at Ricardo's for a facial at one. But thank you for asking." Her eyes beam gratitude as she looks toward Emma.

Impulsively Jane goes up to her and hugs her tightly. "I'll go next time, Mummy, honestly I will."

They hop on a Number 30 double decker bus at Knightsbridge and ride it down past Selfridges and the seething morass of Oxford Street shoppers, getting off at Oxford Circus and walking toward the British Museum, fondly known to everyone in London as 'The BM'.

Bypassing milling clusters of shoppers in the huge museum shop, they make their way through a succession of cavernous exhibition rooms, past a thick knot of onlookers at the Rosetta Stone, eventually arriving at special galleries built for the Elgin Marbles. The exhibition rooms here are enormous with soaring ceilings, suitable for the majesty and grandeur of the fragments of the pediment sculptures from the Parthenon.

Lord Elgin, a diplomat assigned to Greece, salvaged everything he could from the ruins of the Parthenon, when he arrived at his post in Athens. The site had become a giant quarry for marble needed in building construction. The Parthenon also had been the target of attacks in various wars the Greeks periodically engaged in with their enemies, the Turks. Therefore some, Lord Elgin certainly, saw his efforts as an act of preservation. But many in Britain, and the Greeks of course, think the sculptures should be returned. Emma's mind debates these facts as she looks at the sculptures.

They walk around the perimeter of the gallery studying the frieze, low relief sculptures featuring a banquet of the Olympian gods, a battle scene, and a procession. The metope relief sculptures, which would have rested directly beneath the pediment, depict the battle of the Lapiths and Centaurs at the unruly wedding feast. Both girls remember another frieze, at Olympia, featuring the same Battle of the Lapiths and Centaurs, but neither comments. The Olympia museum, and a night spent sobbing into her pillow at the Pensione Anastasia, is still too painful for Jane to talk about.

Finally they look again at the pediment sculptures, massive, larger than life, carved with such verve and animation it is difficult to realize their age, several centuries before the birth of Christ. Emma and Jane gaze silently in admiration.

"How could sculpture that long ago have been so pure, so lifelike?" Jane finally speaks. "It's as though we've been progressing backward, not forward since then. Sculpture done later seems lifeless, unless perhaps, Michelangelo's work. More modern works seem to lack this expertise, this conviction." Her cheeks flush pink.

"Jane," Emma pronounces proudly. "You are well on the road to becoming a great lecturer on the classical age. Remember, I said it first."

Jane tries to hide her pleasure at Emma's words. "Just think, our class resumes soon. And there's another paper to write, before the exam. Have you been thinking about it, Emma? We never even looked at our notes last night after Charlie left."

"I've done a rough draft, nothing more. Maybe we should go to the British Library Reading Room for an hour or so since we are already here at the BM. We could pick up a few reference notes for the papers."

As London University students, they are allowed to use the British Library Reading Room in the BM., a scholar's dream, which draws readers from all over the world. They pick out desks next to each other in the huge domed room, fill in their request slips and hand them over to the attendant. The room is silent save for the subdued rustling of papers and the occasional whisper between readers and clerks, who stagger to deliver armloads of books to the desks.

As Emma waits for her books, she feels a sense of awe, just sitting at a desk beside Jane in the world's most renowned library reading room. I'm sitting here surrounded by some of the mightiest brains in the world, she reflects, looking at the quiet, unassuming scholars at the tables.

When the books arrive they get to work quickly, reading and taking occasional notes. Time passes. Dismayed, Emma looks up at the large clock to see the hands almost reaching three, time for Mrs. Mudge to arrive, and she's completely forgotten until now. Hurriedly she gathers up her papers, stacks the books in a neat tower where they will be collected, and bids Jane a warm, whispered goodbye. Mrs. Mudge has her own key thank goodness. At least she can let herself in.

"Look, Emma, if Mudge can't stay tomorrow night, give me a ring and I'll come stay with you."

A reply is cut off by a loud hissing sound from a stern looking woman near them, wearing a shapeless magenta print and floppy sandals She glowers at them behind enormous spectacles.

Emma meekly nods her thanks to Jane, finger to her lips, and hurries out.

The bus seems to creep up Oxford Street and it is nearly three fifteen when she puts her key in the lock of the flat, ringing the doorbell to let Mrs. Mudge know she is arriving. Unlocking the door to her flat, she hears a drumming, pounding noise from the direction of the kitchen. Running down the hallway, she comes upon a helpless, frustrated and angry Mrs. Mudge, bound and gagged, vehemently beating the floor with her two feet as she sits, tied up like a turkey, in a kitchen chair. Emma runs to her and unties the hateful gag whereupon she begins screaming, "Oh yer villains! I'll get yer, I will! 'Elp! Police!"

Emma checks her over and finds she is unhurt, except for an outraged spirit. She then presses Hawkins' bell and telephones Charlie St. Cyr at Scotland Yard, all the while the background chant of Mrs. Mudge rings out as she rubs her sore wrists and ankles, begging to be "let at" the villains.

"Oh, poor Mrs. Mudge," Emma murmurs, returning to her after a hurried inspection of the flat. She rubs the woman's numbed fingers. "Tell me what happened."

"Two of 'em there was. 'Avin' the nerve to tell me they was 'ere to clean the winders they did. When like a fool I let 'em in, why they grabbed me and tied me up. Then they went to the back of the flat, to your room, Emma, I think. I 'eard 'em rootin' around in there and didn't I start 'ollerin'? They ran back here and put a gag on me right quick, they did, but before they'd got into more mischief yer rang the bell and they scarpered, took off down the drainpipes I reckon. I 'eard 'em raisin' the winder back there."

"I'm so very sorry, Mrs. Mudge," Emma said. "You could have been hurt. Let me get you a cup of tea."

Emma and Mrs. Mudge sit drinking a calming cup of tea when Charlie arrives at the flat. With Hawkins leading the way, they all troop back to Emma's room. An open window and fluttering curtains tell the story, reinforced by a rope tied to the drainpipe and reaching down to the ground, empty now and swaying in the breeze. They didn't have to cope with window screens, Emma silently observes, thankful to be in a country which has eradicated the common house fly. Charlie peers out, but the courtyard is deserted.

Hawkins rushes out the front door and down five flights of stairs to see what he can learn from the courtyard on the ground floor. Emma feels sorry for Hawkins, who is looking decidedly sour; he'd thought his building was an impenetrable fortress. Tight-lipped and in a bad temper, he returns a few minutes later to say that the intruders broke a window in a corridor looking onto the courtyard below in order to make their escape into the vestibule and out the doors onto the street. He admits he was not on duty for a few minutes shortly after three o'clock.

Charlie points to the wide stone window ledge in Emma's room. "Plenty of space to support a man, two men if necessary," he adds. "That's how they got away."

Emma's room is in complete disarray. Drawers upended onto the bed, the wardrobe door hanging open, pictures taken off the walls.

"Your ringing of the bell must have surprised them before they got down to it," Charlie says. "Lucky you got here when you did, Emma."

"Seein' 'er was like seein' an angel," adds Mrs. Mudge gratefully.

Charlie bends over and picks up a folded slip of paper on the carpet under the window. "It must have fallen out of the pocket of one of the men." He unfolds it and reads:

"Lydia went into the room and had a look at her passport. Lives at 34 Chesham Place, S.W.1. She is American. Since it wasn't in the other one's case, it must be in hers. If I get my hands on the idiot who marked the wrong bag, he'll be sorry. Get it! Don't fail us! People here are depending on you." The note was not signed.

"Of course," Emma says, her mind racing furiously. "This must be a letter to Lydia's brother in London, the one who works for the travel agent. He was the one they picked to steal Jane's bag. And he must have been one of the so-called window washers."

"And the father is the owner of the Pensione Anastasia in Olympia?" Charlie asks, his eyes glittering. "What is his name?"

"Give me a second," Emma says, pressing hands to her forehead. "The name was written over the door. P. Leonidas, Proprietor. That's it. The son must be a Michael Leonidas, living in London and working for a travel agent. The waitress Lydia told me about her brother Michael. He's your man."

Charlie moves with lightening speed to the telephone. In a minimum of words he relays the information, confirms his whereabouts and orders a female officer quickly to thirty four Chesham Place.

Mrs. Mudge, somewhat soothed by a good strong cup of tea with three heaping spoonfuls of sugar, is beginning to enjoy herself. What an adventure she has had! Just like it happens on the telly! Emma imagines what must be going through her head.

The stout-hearted Cockney cleaning lady gives Charlie a very good description of the men who bound her up. No, they hadn't bothered to blindfold her, just put a gag over her mouth. Emma smiles, imagining how that lively tongue must have lambasted the intruders before they silenced her.

One of the men, according to Mrs. Mudge was short and wiry with blue eyes and sandy hair. He talked, she said, "just like everybody else." Emma, out of the corner of her eye, notes as Charlie pencils 'Cockney' into his notebook, smiling faintly.

"But that other one was a furriner for sure. Black hair with hairy arms and black eyes. 'E were a rum case if ever I saw one. 'E talked funny too." Emma watched as Charlie wrote 'accent' in his small notebook.

Most people think Cockneys speak a foreign language, Emma muses silently, but Mrs. Mudge, 'born within the sound of Bow Bells,' the East End church of St. Mary Le Beau, as the nursery rhyme declares, is pure Cockney, and more British than anybody. To her, others are the foreigners!

"One of them was probably our Greek travel agent, Mrs. Mudge," Charlie tells her. "Don't you worry, we'll get him. I've already started people looking." Then half-heartedly, almost apologetically, he examines the jumble of Emma's belongings on the bed. "They've already found the amulet if it was in this lot," he says.

"But Charlie, I've searched over every stitch I brought back and there was nothing," Emma sighs, looking with dismay at her belongings which she feels have been defiled.

"These people are amateurs, Emma," he says witheringly. "The right hand doesn't know what the left is doing. When the officer gets here, she'll straighten up everything. You won't have to be around, if you don't want to be. It's her job.

"Now Mrs. Mudge," Charlie turns the full power of his compelling personality on the cleaning lady. "You have performed an invaluable service for Scotland Yard today. Your actions may indeed have far-reaching effects. But we do not want to overtire you. You must go home now and rest. Officer Parsley, one of our best female officers, will be arriving in minutes to take charge here. She will guard Miss Darling and keep her safe. But first I want my officer to drive you safely home. Don't you worry for one minute. And when you are fit and refreshed, if you could just stand by, in case Scotland Yard needs you again?" Charlie smiles his wonderful golden-boy smile and Emma can see Mrs. Mudge transform into a willing slave before her eyes.

"Course I can. Yer can derpend on me."

And she marches proudly out of the flat and into the waiting patrol car, her mind crowded with ever more elaborate versions of her afternoon to relate to 'Enery and the folks at the Bingo, about her dangerous adventure and her important service to Scotland Yard.

Emma and Charlie sit at the kitchen table drinking coffee and waiting for Officer Margery Parsley to return. "Well, what do you think of Mrs. Mudge?" Emma asks.

"She's a trip. Priceless. Larger than life and strong as an ox. Makes me proud I'm British, Emma," Charlie drawls, smiling. "We should have more like her."

"I'm very grateful to her," Emma says. She is indeed a loyal and staunch ally, and a very dangerous enemy," she finishes with a chuckle. "But I do feel sorry for Hawkins. He seems shattered. I think he thought his building was unassailable."

"Well, that myth's been put to rest," Charlie replies. "I suspect Hawkins may have gone to his quarters for fifteen minutes or so of shut-eye," Charlie says, lazily sipping his tea. "Lots of porters do, you know, take that after-lunch nap."

~

Officer Margery Parsley arrives, looking barely sixteen with flaming red hair and a pert and pretty face, an engaging crop of freckles dusting her nose. Her gaze is direct and open under sandy brows. Emma likes her at once. Charlie leaves to track down Michael Leonidas and the two girls go to Emma's room to set things to rights. Emma is weary of the checking and rechecking her belongings.

"But we have to be absolutely sure, don't we, Luv?" says Margery, patiently examining seams, hems, shoulder pads. But they discover nothing. Emma tells the officer she has planned to go out for the evening with a friend.

"Course, Luv, why not? I'm not your jailer, you know. I'll just curl up with a book on a sofa somewhere and be fine."

"And what would you like for your supper?" Emma is thankful the pantry is well-stocked.

"Don't worry, I expect one of my mates will bring me a beef burger from the Wimpy bar in Victoria. Or I can fix some toast and boil an egg. Do you have a tin of beans? I like beans on toast."

Emma assures her that she has, shows her the pantry, then leaves to shower and get ready for Sam.

She takes out a blue linen dress from the wardrobe, a dress that didn't make the cut for Greece because linen wrinkles so easily. But Emma knows it will be perfect for this evening, a special evening with Sam. She slips it over her head and peers in the glass. Tight waist with a flared skirt and a big collar. She knows the color of the dress suits her blonde hair and blue eyes. Will it be raining later? Better get a scarf. She reaches for the blue scarf, suddenly remembering it is not in the bureau drawer, but must be still in the zipper pouch on the outside of her case where Jane stuffed it as they finished their hurried packing at the Pensione Anastasia. But as she reaches for her case on top of the wardrobe, the doorbell rings. Quickly pulling out the scarf, she drops it into her purse, and runs to press the buzzer which will admit Sam to the building.

"Is that you, Sam? Come up in the lift; the flat is on the fifth floor."

Sam's eyes tell her at once how glad he is to see her. "There's someone here you must meet," she says, taking his hand and guiding him through the double doors into the drawing room.

The room has high molded ceilings in the Robert Adam style, a beautifully draped bay window looking down onto Chesham Place. Lights from shaded sconces on the walls cast a soft, golden glow. Officer Parsley, looking attractive in her uniform, stands up to be introduced. It's like the set of an Agatha Christie mystery, Emma thinks admiringly. The perfect setting, with Scotland Yard on the scene.

Emma knows Sam is bursting with questions, but he is much too polite to launch into inquiries until he has exchanged a few pleasantries with Officer Parsley. They say goodbye and close the door.

"Could you possibly tell me what is going on and why a Scotland Yard officer has stationed herself in your flat?" As he speaks he guides her toward Basil Street, behind Harrods, on to Beauchamp Place where the restaurant is located. Emma tells him about the break-in during the afternoon and about Mrs. Mudge being tied up and gagged, and finally about the note found on the bedroom floor.

"And the thieves? Did they catch them?"

"No, not yet, but they at least know who they are looking for. One Michael Leonidas, a son of our pensione owner in Olympia, who lives in London and works for a travel agency in Soho. They're almost certain he's the one who broke into the flat, as the note was obviously sent to him. He had an accomplice, but Charlie St. Cyr, the Scotland Yard detective who is handling the matter, says the accomplice is probably just an acquaintance. He's most likely a Cockney from the East End, Charlie says, after listening to Mrs. Mudge's colorful descriptions of the culprits."

"And how does he know that?" Sam asks.

"Because Mrs. Mudge said one of the pair talked 'just like everybody else', and she's a Cockney born within the sound of Bow Bells if ever there was one. You know the old saying about the church of St. Mary le Beau." Emma grins.

Sam hoots. "What an amazing afternoon you've had, Emma Darling. And the missing amulet?"

"Still missing. The thieves turned out all my things onto the bed, but I arrived before they had time to search everything. Frankly, I've gone over my clothes so many times already I've memorized each buttonhole and stitch. I'm sure the amulet isn't there. I'm beginning to wonder if it really exists."

"Lots of hither and thither going on if it doesn't," Sam says. "And with every move, the conspirators dig themselves into a deeper pit."

"From the very beginning, I thought someone had gone through my things at the Pensione Anastasia," says Emma. "I think they were looking back then for someone to carry the treasure to London. Then came the *baklava* episode with Lydia, the innkeeper's daughter."

"And after that failed someone goofed and marked the wrong case?" Sam asks.

"Apparently so," Emma replies. "At least the note we found seems to suggest that. But how did Michael Leonidas get himself into Heathrow to the baggage claim?"

"Easy as breathing," Sam says. "He's a travel agent, remember. He knows his way around airports, especially that one."

"And when he finally got the case it was the wrong one, because the wrong case was marked. Someone at the Pensione Anastasia made a mistake. Remember there wasn't much time for breakfast before we left on the coach, and there was lots of rushing and confusion. Whoever tried to plant it discovered Jane's bag was already locked, so they slipped it into my case instead. That explains it." Emma feels very pleased with herself.

"Then where is the amulet?" Sam says.

Her smile fades. Where *is* the wretched thing? She has looked through the case twice, then Officer Parsley did her search.

"Perhaps the so-called window cleaners found it after all," Sam sighs. "Well, let's not dwell on it for tonight."

"That suits me fine," Emma agrees, ready to give herself up to enjoyment of the evening.

San Lorenzo, the restaurant Sam has chosen, fills up quickly with a young crowd of diners drifting in as Emma and Sam arrive. They follow their waiter, dressed in white shirt and black trousers, to a banquette in a dim corner of the terrace, surrounded by other tables. Large terra cotta pots filled with white geraniums complete a pleasant setting.

"Pelargoniums you call them, I believe," says Emma, "not just everyday geraniums. My grandmother loved the white ones. This place is charming. How did you happen to choose it, Sam?"

"My pals at Guy's said you'd like it," he answers. "It's supposed to be the restaurant of the moment this summer of 1974, according to the Evening Standard food critic, so I'm told. Whatever that means."

"It means, silly, that it's a lovely spot and people like to go there this summer. The autumn will probably usher in a new restaurant and another location. As for me, I like this one very much. I think I read in the Evening Standard that it's a favorite haunt of Diana Spencer and her pals." She smiles at Sam, worrying a bit about how expensive it appears.

The waiter hands them menus and a wine list. "A glass of Frascati, Emma, or would you prefer *retsina*, evoking memories of Greece? That is, if it's on the wine list." The suspicion of a smile hovers at the corners of Sam's mouth.

"No thank you." Emma says firmly. "Frascati is fine." She has not developed a taste for the resin-flavored wine of Greece.

"A shame, really," says Sam, straight-faced. "I'd planned to order barbecued goat for us and *retsina* would be perfect with it, don't you agree?"

"You wouldn't, you beast," Emma laughs. "Do you know Jane doesn't to this day realize what she really ate that night."

The meal progresses slowly for there is much to talk about. They linger over coffee after a pasta dish and a delicate grilled fish. Their talk covers plans for the coming autumn, leaving the missing amulet out of their leisurely conversation.

"So will you stay on in London this fall?" Emma asks.

"I'm not really certain yet, but I don't think so. My dream has been always to return to Scotland, somewhere not far from Edinburgh, to hang out my shingle in some small village. It would be different from life in London, not so hectic, and my expenses would be a lot less. So would my income! Still, when I think of the attractions, it's what I most want, at least I've thought so in the past."

"That sounds more like my life in Charlottesville," Emma says. "But I must admit, I find city life exciting."

"Oh, you're meant to be in a big city, Emma. I can spot you in my mind at some large museum or gallery. I have trouble picturing you anywhere but London or New York."

This distresses Emma, to be viewed in such a narrow way, but she says nothing. Does he think she couldn't adjust? Steady, Emma, she thinks. This is only a pleasant summer interlude, remember?

The restaurant buzzes with talk and laughter as they leave, walking toward Chesham Place. It begins to sprinkle a little. "I'll get a taxi," Sam offers.

"No, don't. I have a scarf. Let's walk, it isn't far."

She reaches into her shoulder bag and pulls out the scarf. For the first time her fingers touch a lump in one corner, and puzzled, Emma walks closer to a lighted shop window to see better. She unties the knot revealing a smaller lump, something smooth, like a stone, bound up in the corner of the silk.

"What on earth?" she exclaims, unwinding the silk.

A small oval, looking like an oversize charm, about four inches in length, lies in the folds. It is made of alabaster or marble, carved in low relief. Looking more closely she makes out the figure of a Greek god, Apollo, surely. Sam is by now peering over her shoulder. He whistles. Emma gasps in astonishment. How could she have missed it in the outside pocket of her suitcase when she searched all those times? And how could she have to failed to search that outside pocket, where she remembers now, Jane thrust her scarf during the frenzy of packing? And she didn't even feel it earlier when she hastily grabbed the scarf as Sam rang the bell to the flat!

"You've found the missing Apollo Amulet, Emma," Sam whispers, placing his arms around her, unmindful of strollers and window shoppers along Beauchamp Place.

He embraces her, then quickly they make their way toward Chesham Place in the calm of a misty summer evening.

SIX

From Belgravia to Soho to the Earls Court Road

Officer Parsley is idly thumbing through the satire-laden pages of a Private Eye magazine when Sam and Emma hurry into the flat.

"I didn't expect you back so soon." she says, standing up.

"Look here, Margery!" With shaking hands Emma unwraps the scarf and displays the amulet. Surrounded by the folds of the silk, it shines and glimmers.

"Cor! Looks like you struck gold! Where did you find that?"

Emma quickly tells her, and Officer Parsley hurries to the telephone, ringing Charlie's number. In no time at all, it seems, he is standing at the door of the flat, waiting to be let in. Emma greets him warmly and begins relating events, after first introducing him to Sam.

"Jane wore my scarf in Olympia. When she discovered it just before we left, I'd already closed and locked my case. I was afraid I couldn't close it if I reopened it, so she stuffed it in the outside zipper pouch. Shortly after that we hurried downstairs for a quick breakfast. The cases were picked up and loaded onto the coach as we ate. I forgot all about the scarf in there."

Sam takes up the story. "Then someone, realizing both cases were locked, tied the amulet in the corner of the scarf, jammed it back in the outside pocket where they'd found it. It was all they could do, even though Jane's case bore the special column mark. They were desperate to get it away to London, you see. They had looked at your passport earlier Emma, you told me that they knew your London address." Emma nods.

"Unfortunately," Charlie takes up the threads, "it was too late to get word to the contact man in London, or perhaps they tried and failed; at any rate, he picks up the marked bag at Heathrow as he'd been told to do. Spotting a marked bag is much quicker than trying to read two hundred labels going around a carousel."

"He must have been in a right state when he got to the men's room with Jane's case, went through it and found nothing," Sam reflects, grinning at Charlie. The two men are getting on famously, Emma notices.

"So he rips off the identification," Charlie resumes, "hoping the bag won't go to the owner and arouse suspicion, but at the same time, not wanting to be branded as a thief. Only Jane's careful description of her case and an extremely alert baggage handler, Mr. Patel, saved the day and got Jane's case back to her."

Emma looks up quickly. "You contacted Heathrow baggage?"

Charlie nods as if to say, "Do you think I'm a twit? Don't you think we do our job?"

"Meanwhile," Sam continues, "The thief, the nephew travel agent, knows he's failed in his mission. He puts in a quick call to his father at Pensione Anastasia in Olympia for instructions. I imagine the gist of what he was told was taken down in the form of a note which dropped out of his pocket onto Emma's bedroom floor when he made a hurried escape down the rope from her flat."

Emma's eyebrows fly up. "Is that what you think, Charlie?"

"Probably." Charlie answers cautiously. "Remember the nephew has to be very careful. He knows England has much tighter police surveillance than his native Greece. He doesn't want to get into trouble and face being deported. He possibly hired an off-duty window cleaner to do the job with him. As he accompanied the bona fide window cleaner, he must have faced sheer terror when he had to exit the flat by a rope five floors up."

"Perching on the ledge, then going down. Yes, it would have been harrowing to someone not used to heights," Sam muses.

They are sitting around the pine table in the kitchen, drinking coffee made by Officer Parsley. The amulet is in the center of the table, nestling in the folds of the blue scarf. Emma studies it carefully.

The figure of Apollo is standing, face turned in profile, his left arm raised, folds of his cloak falling in a graceful drape, tapering toward the back, the garment loosely belted at the waist, ending at the knees. He wears a warrior's helmet and high laced sandals. His nose is straight; a few curls peep beneath the helmet. An arresting figure.

"Could the stone be alabaster?" Sam asks.

"Maybe," Emma says. "Although it's been polished enough to look like a precious jewel. Charlie," Emma asks on an impulse, "why can't I ring Jane? She will be so excited to know we've found it. Surely she should see it, before you take it away. You *are* going to take it away, aren't you?"

Charlie hesitates for a moment. "Yes, I'm going to take it away, and yes, of course she would like to see it, before we turn it over to the British Museum experts. I'll send officer Parsley over in the car to pick her up, if she'll come."

~

Jane quickly climbs into a pair of dungarees and a plaid shirt after Emma's call. Her face is flushed pink from sleep when she arrives at the flat with officer Parsley. She looks intently at the amulet for some moments.

She gazes at the stone's rosy surface musing, "What stories it could tell us if it could only speak."

"We've still a way to go," Charlie says softly, as though speaking to her alone. "Lots of unanswered questions."

"What do you mean?" Emma asks.

"Well, I hate to admit it, but we haven't found young Leonidas yet."

"But surely he wouldn't be that hard to trace," Emma persists. "Not with that name."

"There are lots of Greeks living in London, Emma. And, we have traced him, just haven't located him. He's a travel agent at the Grecian Isles Travel Agency at fifty three Charlotte Street. Trouble is, he hasn't been at work for a couple of days and his rooms over the agency are empty. Mr. Leonidas has taken a sudden, unexplained leave of absence. Nobody seems to know where he is or where he's gone, but his possessions are still in his rooms."

Emma's brain is working furiously. Where could Mike Leonidas be hiding? They must find him; he is the key. He can fill in all the blanks about who actually masterminded the plot to steal the amulet, and who killed the Bassae Shepherd. They must be sure that the shepherd did not die in vain.

Jane speaks up suddenly. "Has anyone considered the possibility that the amulet might not be authentic?"

Her words have the shattering effect of a bomb going off. Emma looks at her in amazement, her heart sinking.

"Do you really think it might be a fake? The carving is so beautiful."

"I don't know for certain of course," Jane replies timidly, "it just strikes me that it's in awfully good condition to have that much age on it. And I'm not certain it's alabaster, either. I would guess it's cornelian, a pale-coloured variety of course. And take the helmet: it seems slightly more like the helmets on Roman relief sculptures rather than Greek." She blushes furiously and sits back in her chair, anxious because she knows what she has just said disappoints them.

Sam presses his fingers together saying nothing. Charlie, deflated by her words, appears swayed by her reasoning. As for Emma, she has no doubts, what Jane says must be correct. Jane knows more than anyone about the Greek period. She trusts her friend's perspicacity.

"Maybe we should call Miss Crawford." Sam says suddenly. "She's bound to want to know about this. And she is an expert of course."

Jane pales and Emma, seeing her friend's discomfort, murmurs something about the lateness of the hour. After the debacle at Olympia, Jane still feels the hurt of that disaster, Emma realizes.

But Charlie hails Sam's suggestion as a splendid idea. He doesn't think it is too late, after such an obviously important discovery. And he would like very much to know her opinion of the amulet's authenticity.

"I have her telephone number. I'll just give a tinkle."

Emma and Jane exchange glances. No doubt he charmed the university secretary into getting whatever information he wanted, such as Miss Crawford's personal telephone number. And apparently Scotland Yard makes calls on the telephone, or in person, any time of the day or night they wish!

While Jane and Emma hold their breaths, Charlie confidently dials Maria Crawford's number at her home. After four double rings, they hear the distinctly frosty voice of their teacher. "Yes?"

Charlie immediately identifies himself, apologizing for the late hour then telling her the reason for his call. Miss Crawford's clarion voice rings out, audible to all as she expresses a pleased surprise, frosty voice warming in a twinkling.

"Yes indeed," Charlie continues smoothly, "I knew you would be delighted to hear it had been found and I thought perhaps you might wish to see it before it's tucked away for safekeeping and examined by the BM jewel experts."

He adds a sentence about her splendid efforts on behalf of the Bassae Shepherd and the Greek art ministry. Smoothly, sincerely, he's laying it on with a trowel, Emma thinks, listening with admiration.

"I thought you might," Charlie agrees, nodding. "We are at the flat of Miss Emma Darling on Chesham Place, S.W.1. I'll send an officer in a car to collect you. Will twenty minutes be all right? Yes, fine. I remember, 242 Russell Square. Right. Goodbye." Like a cat who's been at the cream jug, Charlie puts down the telephone.

"She's coming." Emma can hardly believe it, glancing nervously around the kitchen.

She flies to the door when the buzzer sounds, meeting them at the door as officer Parsley ushers Miss Crawford into the flat. She is wearing a dark, flowing dress of indeterminate style, suede house slippers and no jewelry, her concession to the hour. She steps into the pool of light around the kitchen table and greets them all.

"Thank you so much for coming." Charlie warmly shakes her hand.

Charlie is at his most engaging after greetings are exchanged around the table. Briefly he summarizes in a few words the whereabouts of the amulet, how it left Greece. Miss Crawford listens intently, then turns her attention to the amulet before her. For several minutes she scrutinizes it, asking if she might touch it. Charlie nods, and silently, she turns it over in her long, slim fingers.

"Of course, the inscription on the back reads 'Phidias made me'." At once Emma's hopes rise. Maybe it is the original after all, thinking of the recent discovery of the great sculptor's tea mug, in the ruins of Olympia.

"Surely that means it's genuine," Emma whispers, voice barely audible, her fingers nervously twisting the fringe of the tablecloth.

Sam places a hand on her arm. "Not necessarily," he says softly.

Miss Crawford continues to examine the amulet. Finally she raises her eyes and looks at everyone ranged around the table as tension in the room rises. Emma rubs her moist palms. Jane looks frozen, mouth pressed in a thin line.

At last Maria Crawford speaks. "The stone of course, is cornelian, not the alabaster which we would have expected had the piece been by Phidias's hand. We know the ancient Greeks worked in alabaster as well as marble, particularly in small, precious pieces like this.

"Secondly, the helmet is of a Roman type, not Greek. If you look at the way the visor is attached and at the shape of the crown, you will quickly see what I mean. Think of Athena's helmet you saw over and over again in Greek sculptures recently," here she looks at Sam, Emma and Jane, addressing them as students. "Those helmets had much more shallow crowns.

"Thirdly, the condition of the piece leads me to believe it is an 18th century copy of a Greek original, the original quite possibly made by Phidias himself. This appears to be a copy, perhaps made by a Neapolitan cameo artisan working where or from what inspiration we do not, unfortunately, know. Nor do we know how such a piece found its way to the Bassae area where it was secreted for so many years. That is my on-the-spot opinion. Of course the experts can subject the piece to certain scientific tests and come up with a more definite analysis."

Emma can hardly contain herself. What Miss Crawford has just said is, in essence, just what Jane told them earlier. But she lacks the courage to speak up.

"In other words, it's a fake," Charlie says flatly.

"Not necessarily a fake," Sam offers. "A rather beautiful copy of an ancient work of art now perhaps lost forever. It is a thing of beauty in its own right."

"Well said, Sam," Miss Crawford beams. "How very perceptive of you."

"And not just Dr. McGregor," Charlie speaks up. "Miss Hale looked at the amulet before you arrived and expressed the identical opinion about the origin of the piece." Silently Emma cheers; only Charlie, who is unaware of the earlier episode in the Olympia museum, would dare to give credit to someone else, especially Jane.

"Oh, no," Jane speaks up. "I didn't have any idea who could have made the piece. I don't know any Greek, and I didn't know it's possible date. I just mentioned it might be cornelian and that the helmet somehow looked more Roman than Greek. That's all."

If she could disappear into the wall-paper like the ladies in Bonnard's paintings of Parisian interiors, she would melt away right this minute, Emma thinks, loyally applauding Jane's modesty in silence.

"Yes, well," Miss Crawford replies generously, "Jane is of course one of my most gifted students. I am not surprised she came to this conclusion." She raises her hand. "Now I caution you. I am no expert on amulets. I may be wrong entirely. The BM experts in this field will give us a much clearer picture when they get their hands on it."

But nobody in the room doubts her analysis will prove accurate.

~

Filled with misgivings the next afternoon, Emma takes the tube to Soho and gets off at Leicester Square. She slept very late the morning after the discovery of the amulet, a sleep troubled by dreams. In one dream a shadowy figure reappears again and again. He is featureless, but in her mind the figure becomes Michael Leonidas, the missing travel agent Charlie and the operatives of Scotland Yard are searching for.

As she dressed and ate a hurried breakfast, the conviction that this man must be the one to unlock the secrets of the amulet grew stronger, and when Officer Parsley left the flat to go back to Scotland Yard until later in the evening when she will return, Emma made up her mind. She would go to Charlotte Street to glean clues about the missing man.

As she crosses into Charlotte Street, the hot breath of a bus puffs around her legs as she walks. Charlotte street reminds her of a gigantic kitchen with aromatic smells issuing forth from the variety of ethnic food shops and restaurants lining the street. She passes the upscale Bertorelli's Italian restaurant, The White House, a well-known Greek dining spot, but there are smaller premises where, if one chooses, one may dine on Chinese, Cypriot, Greek or even more exotic middle eastern fare. Emma inhales the tantalizing aroma of meat roasting on giant spits for falafel and kebabs.

Number fifty-three is a small, unpromising storefront with a dusty sign in the window proclaiming Grecian Isles Travel. A few shopworn posters boast glories of the Acropolis and the Parthenon, Corfu, Crete, Delphi. That is the extent of window dressing. Emma goes inside to find only one person in attendance, a thin, nervous looking girl with dark hair and eyes, carefully applying dark red nail varnish to her fingernails.

"Yes?" she inquires listlessly, blowing on the nails to dry them more quickly. "May I help you?"

"I am interested in booking a tour to Greece," Emma announces boldly, hoping she sounds convincing.

"It's not a good time of the year to travel there, you know," the girl answers surprisingly. "It's very hot in Greece now." The girl screws on the bottle cap of the nail varnish. Her dark hair is long and lustrous, but the expression in her eyes seems sad.

"I see," Emma says. "Then when would you suggest?"

"Sometime after August. Then the heat becomes more bearable." She looks carefully at Emma.

"You must be a native of Greece," Emma says pleasantly to the girl. "You sound like you know the climate very well there."

The girl shrugs. "I'm from Athens. When you live there, you don't notice it. But I'm more used to this cooler climate now."

This can go on forever, thinks Emma. How on earth am I going to get round to Mike Leonidas? She decides to try the direct approach.

"Listen Alexis," she says in a soft voice, glancing at the girl's name, Alexis Sobranos, on a plaque on her desk, "I'm not here to buy a ticket to Athens. What I really want to know is, where is Mike Leonidas?"

The girl draws back immediately, dark eyes narrowing, her face scowling like a sudden ocean squall. "You are the police, aren't you? I knew they would be back again for Mike." Suddenly the carefully made-up face dissolves in a rush of tears. Dismayed, Emma answers quickly.

"No, Alexis. I'm not the police. I'm Emma Darling, an American student in London for a year, studying art history. I was in Greece recently, and I met Lydia, Mike's sister, that's all." Alexis dries her eyes, looks at her.

"Honestly, it's true." Emma rushes on. "I know about the missing amulet. I wanted to talk to Mike, to tell him the good news that the amulet's been found. I wanted to try to convince him to go to the police and tell them everything he knows." Her words tumble out in a rush. The girl Alexis is clearly not putting on an act. She is worried sick.

"Then the amulet has been found? Thank goodness. You would talk to him, try to convince him to go to the police?" Alexis looks hopefully into Emma's eyes.

"Yes, I will. I really want to help him." Emma's eyes plead with as much conviction as she can muster.

Emma leans back, hands in her lap, silently watching Alexis, not wanting to reveal more than is necessary to get information. *I'm probably already in a lot of hot water with Charlie for striking out on my own. And Sam?* Emma quakes inwardly, knowing Sam won't approve of what she is doing. *Let the police handle this.* Emma can almost hear him saying it.

"If you knew how many times I have tried to get him to go to the police! Mike is innocent, but I tell him, as long as he hides, the police will think he is guilty. Why can't he see that? He only did what his father ordered him to do. Wouldn't an obedient son obey the commands of his father?" Alexis Sobranos halts as though she is afraid of her own words.

He has told her to keep quiet, Emma realizes. She feels a little frisson of fear. *Do I really want to confront a desperate man? It might put me in danger.* But she keeps her countenance calm.

"Where will I find him, Alexis?" she asks, coming to a decision about her role in unraveling the mystery of the amulet: she will try to discover the truth.

"At my flat in the Earls Court Road," Alexis answers, deciding on impulse to trust this forthright American girl. "I'll take you to him if you like."

"All right," Emma says, "but first I must call a friend and tell her I'll be late for our meeting." Alexis points to the telephone. Quickly Emma dials Jane's number.

"Felicity here. Is that you, Rupert?" Jane's mother's fluty voice fills the room. Emma's heart sinks. I must give her a message Jane will understand, Emma thinks desperately.

"Mrs. Hale? Emma Darling here. Could you possibly give a message to Jane? Please tell her that I'm not going to be able to come over until I've made a visit to Twenty Four Earls Court Road. I should be back by seven. Tell her I'll ring her then, would you?" Please, Felicity, don't muddle this, Emma pleads wordlessly, willing Felicity to get it right. Her safety may depend on it.

"You say you'll be at Twenty Four Earls Court Road? Back by seven? Will ring then? Got it! I'll deliver the message, Pet!"

There, thinks Emma, putting down the telephone. Jane will know we hadn't planned to meet at all; she'll realize I'm telling her where I'll be, in case, well, in case I need help. Jane will know to call Charlie. On the other hand, I can talk with Mike Leonidas and return home by seven and ring Jane to say all is well. She takes a deep breath and turns to Alexis.

"Let's go."

Alexis has already tidied her desk, hung the 'CLOSED' sign on the door and is ready to lock up, explaining, "It's almost closing time and Mr. Costas, the owner, has gone for the day. He won't mind if I leave a little early, I don't make a habit of it."

"What does he think of Mike's unexplained absence?" Emma asks as they leave.

"He doesn't like it one bit," Alexis answers quickly, frowning. "I'm afraid Mike will lose his job if he isn't careful."

They take the tube to Earls Court Road, emerging into the bustle of another of London's ethnic neighborhoods, rich with color, sound and smell. Indian women wearing graceful saris look like enormous exotic birds in brilliant plumage as they walk gracefully down the high street. Dark Africans wearing the fez and voluminous trousers; long-limbed, shorts-clad Australians, faces burned by the sun. All mingle on the Earls Court Road. It is an area of cheap lodgings and attracts immigrants, tourists and newcomers.

Number twenty-four is a tired house in a row of houses, all of which once knew better days. Of pleasing proportions, it has become a lodging house of tiny flats, and its walls thirst for a fresh coat of paint. It stands next to a building which has been transformed a brilliant shade of yellow, cheerful, but jarring to the eyes. Beside the front door hang a profusion of doorbells. One is labeled 'A. Sobranos' Emma notes. Alexis Sobranos is telling the truth.

Alex opens the front door with her key. No luxury of a porter here, Emma thinks, trying to imagine Hawkins presiding over such an unworthy address. It is beyond her capabilities, however, to picture him in such a setting.

They enter what has once been a spacious reception hallway, now transformed into a garage for mopeds and bicycles. Vehicles of varying age and condition are propped against walls, rest on stands, barely leaving a pathway to a staircase with beautiful, old wooden balusters and a balustrade polished with the rubbing of many moving hands through the years. There is no lift.

"I'll go first," says Alexis, leading the way. "I'm on the first floor."

Ah yes, Emma thinks. In England the ground floor is the ground floor. Just so. First floor up is the first floor, not the second floor, like it is back home. Alexis unlocks the door of her flat which looks down on to the busy road below.

The flat they enter is a bed-sitter, one room containing a single bed, a kitchen area partitioned from the rest of the room by a beaded curtain and, facing the Earls Court Road, a large bay widow needing the touch of a window cleaner.

An ancient sofa and two rigid arm chairs whose threadbare upholstery faintly reveals lush sprays of faded cabbage roses. This completes the sparsely furnished space. The room is very clean, however. Emma is touched by the circumstances in which so many people live. Here life offers few luxuries, yet pride remains. A slight rustle behind the curtains catches her attention.

"Mike," Alexis calls. "I've brought a friend to see you."

Cautiously parting the curtains, a thin, swarthy, unshaven young man of about twenty two steps forward warily. He does not look pleased.

"What have you done, Alex?"

Emma swallows, hoping she can be convincing and persuasive in her mission. She knows she must not fail.

"Relax, Mike, you are on edge. This is Emma Darling, an American who knows your sister Lydia. Believe me, she wants to help you."

"Of all the people in the world, you have to bring in the one person I'm most ashamed to see." Advancing toward the little sitting area, Mike Leonidas slouches into one of the old chairs, puts his head in his hands. "Didn't I tell you, Alex?" he moans. "She's the girl whose flat I searched." His voice holds despair.

Emma steps forward. "I know how that happened, Mike. It really was not your idea, was it? And I think I can help you. That's why I'm here. Believe me, all is not lost."

He looks up at her glumly. "So you are Emma Darling. Just how do you think you can help me? How can anybody help me now?" Again he puts his head in his hands. Never has Emma seen such despair.

Her heart goes out to Michael Leonidas at that moment, and she resolves to try to shift the tremendous weight of guilt from his thin shoulders. For the first time she understands how a victim who is weak, hoping to avoid unpleasantness, can become entangled in a web of wrong-doing and deceit, hating it and regretting it, but unable to extricate himself. And Alexis! She has risked the security of her job for Mike, no doubt making excuses for his absences, trying to set things right. Obviously she has invested a great deal in Mike. Emma resolves to help if she can.

SEVEN

Uncle Scopas Pays a Call

A melancholy Mike Leonidas tells Emma his story as they sit with Alexis Sobranos in the bed-sitter on the Earls Court Road. It is not a pretty story, but not one without hope. Petrus Leonidas, his father, possessed a will strong enough to try to lift himself and his family from a life of the cruelest poverty. He started as a waiter, a porter and jack of all trades, employed at the Pensione Anastasia. Diligent and energetic, he eventually saved enough to buy a small interest in the place whose absentee owner in Athens had begun thinking of selling the business.

Sudden financial demands caused the owner to make a quick and unexpected offer of sale. Petrus, at great hardship to himself and his family, managed to scrape together a portion of the money. He gave a note to the seller, a promise to pay the remaining amount in ten years. His immediate dream of owning his own property was realized, and he set about redoubling his efforts, his goal to improve the property and increase his income.

His wife took over the kitchen, his younger children did whatever they could to help. His oldest son Michael was his mainstay. The little pensione prospered. The note was paid. Then Mike begged his father for permission to go to London to find a job as a travel agent. He persuaded his father he could help by referring tourists bound for Greece to Pensione Anastasia. His father consented, hoping his son would bring honor to his family as well as more tourists to his pensione.

Meanwhile, the father's older brother, Scopas, still a herder in the hills near Olympia, had become a passionate supporter of the Greek-Cypriot cause and a member of a radical faction trying to drive all Turks out of Cyprus by force and make the island a part of Greece. As older brother, Scopas became titular head of the family when the father died and lost no time in trying to force his younger brother to become active in the cause.

It was Scopas who persuaded Petrus Leonidas to become entangled in a dangerous enterprise. When members of the Greek-Cypriot group uncovered the hiding place of the ancient amulet, secreted for many years in the hills near Bassae, they hatched a plan to steal it. Next they demanded Petrus order his son to help them by taking it to an underground art dealer in London and selling it. They knew it would bring a considerable amount of money, money they needed urgently to fuel their political cause. Petrus became an unwilling accomplice in this plan.

"My father was afraid when they came to demand help," Mike says, shaking his head. "He knew what they were engaged in was wrong, he wanted no part of it. But Scopas was very clever: he put into play the principle of family loyalty, told my father he owed allegiance to him, as head of our family."

He looks earnestly over at Emma, sitting across from him. "You have to understand, the sense of loyalty to family is very strong in Greece, stronger than most anything else, really. Reluctantly my father agreed. He would help get the amulet to London; a group of students from London were staying at the Pensione Anastasia at that very moment. He thought that he could arrange something. Then I would take it to the right person in London who would sell it, and that would be the end of our participation. You have to know, that is what we planned." Emma nods as Michael Leonidas takes a deep breath and continues his story.

"You know what happens next, the mix-up and a whole string of disasters, finishing with me posing as a window cleaner at your flat. Those telephone calls with nobody on the line, the note dropped through the letterbox, they were all meant to soften you up so that you wouldn't put up a fight when we found the amulet and tried to take it away. The mate who went with me was a real window cleaner. He knew nothing about the plan. He knew how to shimmy down that rope five floors. I nearly ruined my hands, burning them as I slid down." Here he holds up his red, swollen palms to show her. Emma winces, seeing them.

"Back in Greece, they decided that you would be the best bet to carry the amulet, because of your American passport. They thought American police wouldn't bother them like Scotland Yard if we got into trouble in London. Ha. And Scotland Yard got into it real quick anyhow, didn't they?" Mike shakes his head ruefully.

"Well, as you know, the amulet didn't turn up in the suitcase at the airport. I'd yanked the case off the carousel real quick when I saw the marking of a column on it. That was the sign they told me to look for. But there was nothing looking like the amulet inside. I telephoned my father and he told Scopas who sent me a telegram ordering me to go to your flat and search. He said the political group would take it out on my family at the pensione if I didn't do as he said. Then my father telephoned me again, begging me to go along with Scopas, the old family loyalty thing again, so what choice did I have?" Sadly he looks at his scarred palms.

"My father said after I did my part, then we could get out of it. I don't think so, but I didn't tell him that. I think Scopas would have kept making more and more demands on us, threats against my mother, my sister, whoever. There would have been no end to the misery. I'll be glad when the amulet is found. I'm telling you, I'll be really glad."

Emma shifts uneasily in her chair. She wants Charlie to be the one to tell Mike the amulet has been found. Charlie will surely want her to keep that fact secret if at all possible. Emma glances quickly at Alex. Why did I have to mention it to her? But Alex meets her glance and is silent. *She's letting me do it my way.*

"Then we ran into that harridan at your flat," Mike continues his story. "She was a Nosy Parker all right, following us around. She knew from the minute she let us in we weren't really there to wash windows. And she didn't waste a second telling us so, either. And loud? You haven't a clue! We finally had to tie her up and put a gag on her, else she would have alerted the whole of the West End!" Emma smiles secretly. *Praise be for Mrs. Mudge!*

"But by the time we got to the back bedroom to begin our search, you rang the doorbell and put your key in the lock. We had to drop everything and scarper quick as all get out. We left by the window in your bedroom, shimmying down five floors on a rope. That's what we did in the confusion while you were freeing up that wild Cockney lady. We were rattled, I tell you. It's a wonder I made it down at all." He glances again at his hands.

"It was then I decided I'd better drop out for a while. Alex said I could stay on her sofa for a few days and keep hidden. Frankly I was scared of what Uncle Scopas would do when he found out we'd failed again to get the amulet. And to top it all off, I probably won't have a job anymore, I've been absent so much." He sighs.

Emma feels sorry for Mike. He is not a bad person. He's been caught up in events beyond his control, and has suffered the consequences.

"And what about the Bassae Shepherd? What about George Soutakis?" Emma asks in a quiet voice.

His face is puzzled. "Who?" he said. "I don't know any Bassae Shepherd, or George Soutakis either, for that matter."

Relieved, Emma believes he is telling the truth. I know I'm gullible, she thinks, but I believe him. His uncle and his father kept that from him. They realized it would frighten Mike, perhaps cause him to desert the cause completely.

Slowly, briefly and succinctly, Emma relates the known details about the Bassae Shepherd, George Soutakis. The man who tried so hard to save the amulet for his country. And lost his life in the effort. As she finishes telling of the hit and run accident on Constitution Square, Mike becomes extremely agitated.

"This means it's over for me," he moans. "I'll be tied to a murder, now. They'll ship me back to Greece and I'll spend the rest of my life in prison."

"But don't you see, Mike?" Emma speaks up quickly. "This is why you must go to the police, and give yourself up. You must tell them everything you know. I believe you are telling the truth when you say you didn't know anything at all about the Bassae Shepherd. The police will believe you too. You must go to them so you can help your father, your mother and your brothers and Lydia. Get them out from under Scopas's heel." Emma clenches her fists, willing him to understand.

The silence in the room lasts only seconds but it seems like forever to Emma.

"All right," Mike says quietly. "I'll go. I'm sick of all the hiding. I don't care what happens to me."

Emma feels limp with relief. He will turn himself in. Alexis too, looks happier than Emma has seen her all afternoon. Emma realizes that this quiet girl cares deeply about what happens to Mike Leonidas. She has a big stake the outcome of the saga.

Emma glances at her watch. Already a quarter before seven. She must call Jane to let her know she is all right, tell her she will be back home soon.

"I need to make a quick telephone call from the call box at the stairs."

But before she rises to her feet, a loud knock sounds. Alexis frowns, her hands begin to tremble as she motions to Mike to hide behind the curtain. She goes to the door.

"Open up at once," a voice thunders, menacing. Alexis opens the door and a short. muscular, bearded man wearing a black sailor's cap with a visor bustles in.

"Where is my nephew, Michael Leonidas?" he demands in a heavily accented, threatening voice.

"Uncle Scopas?" Mike blurts out, coming from behind the beaded curtain. "What in the world are you doing in London?"

"I have come here to take charge of everything."

The brash, swaggering figure, barely five feet with bulging forearms spilling out of a black sweater, bawls the words, looking with displeasure at his nephew.

I know the type, Emma thinks. All bluster and accusation without bothering to hear any of the facts.

"So far you have failed at every turn," the man continues. "I am here to change all of that." He seems to swell up like a rooster in his self-importance. Emma hides a smile.

"Who are these women?" he demands, his eyes grating over first Alex, then Emma.

That look of insolence makes Emma feel as though she is a detail, an afterthought, like a piece of the discarded, make-shift furniture in the mean room on the Earls Court Road. Emma feels her hackles rise. She has seen that look before, in Greece, on the faces of men lounging at *taverna* tables while the women do all of the work. She resolves to be just as difficult and stubborn as she can.

"Uncle," Mike answers, "this is Alexis Sobranos who lives here in this flat. She works at the travel agency where I work." He nods toward Alexis who stands near Emma.

"Yes, yes, I know all that," Scopas answers impatiently. "Why do you think I'm here? Her employer gave me her address when I telephoned him this morning and told him I was her cousin and wanted to surprise her." Scopas turns toward Emma. "And this one?" His voice is dismissive.

Before Mike can answer Emma speaks up quickly. "I am Emma Darling, an American student living in London, under the full protection of the American Embassy."

As soon as the words fall from her mouth Emma wonders why she has been so abrasive. Something about the man inspires contempt. She wants to put him down. But is it wise?

"So you are the one who has been causing all the trouble. Where is the amulet?"

Emma imagines Scopas is twisting her wrist even before he advances a step. His eyes bore into hers, but she stands her ground and resolves to say nothing.

"So that is the way it is." Scopas spits out the words nastily, stepping closer.

"Why do you think I should know?" She answers with contempt, asking a question of her own. And she looks him straight in the eye.

"So that is the way you jump! Do not play games with me, little rich-girl American. We have ways in Greece to make people talk." His face darkens and his eyes take on ugly glints. His voice lowers a few decibels.

Emma feels fear for the first time. This could become very unpleasant she realizes, wondering if she can count on Mike to come to her aid, then deciding it mustn't come to that, whatever happens. There will be no more violence.

"Uncle!" Mike breaks in, "she is trying to help." Alexis stands by the door, frozen in space, looking like some startled gazelle who will bolt at any minute. Mike's face has turned the color of wet concrete; he knows his uncle can be dangerous.

"Where is the amulet?" Scopas faces her again. "I am not a patient man."

Emma counters with another question, "What about George Soutakis? What about his hit-and-run death?"

Scopas narrows his eyes and looks at her. Emma discerns a flicker of fear in his rodent-like face. "I know nothing about that crazy man's death, I tell you. Nothing at all." Then he takes another step forward and puts up his hands as though to grasp her throat.

Danger. The word flashes through Emma's mind as she prepares to defend herself. She opens her mouth to emit a scream of shattering intensity. Alexis, immobilized by fear, quickly takes a giant step toward Emma throwing an arm around her shoulders.

Mike Leonidas jumps, moving toward his uncle as though to tackle him. But a tiny click at the door surprises them all as Charlie St. Cyr glides into the room, all calmness and cool, his impeccably tailored, double breasted suit with side vents and a coordinating silk tie, a mute, understated tribute to his Savile Row tailor.

"Shall we just calm down a few minutes everyone, and not get overwrought? Then we can discuss things sensibly."

Charlie's manner, so assured, so relaxed, they might have been gathering at the Fortnum and Mason Provisions counter, discussing the merits of various cheeses, or maybe sitting in the refreshment tent at Wimbledon, Emma imagines wildly, talking over a tennis match just played while nibbling at strawberries and cream. Emma allows her fancy to take flight, so delighted and relieved is she at Charlie's appearance.

Scopas is clearly puzzled, not a glimmer of light there as to what is happening. Mike seems to guess the identity of the surprise visitor. He looks visibly encouraged, obviously preferring to end up in the hands of Scotland Yard rather than face the wrath of his Greek uncle. For Alexis, Charlie is a welcome apparition, a guardian angel arriving just in the nick of time.

Emma, her powerful imagination fine tuned, can still feel those grubby hands closing on her throat. Thankfully she feels the tension inside begin to dissolve.

"Now everybody calm down and take a seat, please. We'll talk things over in a reasonable way."

Charlie speaks as two uniformed policemen silently materialize inside the flat, placing themselves on either side of Scopas. The rubber band eases more in Emma's stomach.

~

Later that evening, after saying goodbye to Officer Margery Parsley who is returning to her Scotland Yard office now that the danger is over, Emma sits tucked up in bed, enjoying a quiet evening, her first in several days. Charlie has the Apollo Amulet safe in the vaults of Scotland Yard, Uncle Scopas is in custody. There is nothing left to worry about. She knows Mike Leonidas will do her no harm. With a sigh she realizes the excitement of recent days will now subside. Life will rock along, for a change, at its inevitable and pleasant pace.

Beside her on the covers lies a thick, fat letter to Crozet in which she tells her family of the adventure in which she has so recently become entangled. The version has been somewhat downgraded; she knows her parents worry about her, even though she is twenty three. I guess that is the lot of parents, she thinks, eternally worrying about their offspring. She turns off the light and prepares her thoughts for sleep. She realizes she will face an explosion when Sam is informed of the wild events at Earls Court Road. She smiles to herself. At least, if he explodes, it will mean he cares.

Two days after the Earls Court Road occurrence, Emma is in the kitchen idly reading the morning Telegraph. Rain falls steadily outside the double windows, rain in heavy, leaden sheets. Not a morning for venturing out unless absolutely necessary. She pours another cup of coffee.

She realizes there would have been an entirely different ending to the story had not Charlie St. Cyr appeared on the scene just when things began getting out of hand. What a relief he showed up, and took charge of Scopas. He knew exactly what to say to Mike too. Not that she had feared Mike. She had believed in his innocence, but she knows Michael Leonidas is weak. It's been difficult for him having such a domineering family.

Idly she wonders how long Mike would have stood up to his uncle, if Charlie hadn't come along. What if Scopas tried to extract information from her by force? At what point would she have lost her nerve? She sighs, thinking for the hundredth time how glad she is Felicity Hale delivered the message, Jane picked up on it and rang Charlie immediately, not waiting until seven o'clock.

In retrospect, was I foolish to go, Emma wonders? I know it was dangerous. It was just that I felt so strongly after meeting Alexis that Mike needed to give up and go to the police. I had to try to persuade him.

But what had impelled her to go in the first place? Her mind maunders over this, but she can come up with no ready answer. As she continues gazing out at the rain, the thought presents itself that she wants somehow to avenge the shepherd's death. The Bassae Shepherd tried valiantly to protect the amulet, to save it for his homeland. I don't want him to give his life for nothing, she whispers. *He deserves more than that.*

Jane was the first person she had rung when she was safe in her flat again. Jane told her she'd become frightened when Felicity told her about Emma's message. She knew Emma was signaling to her because they hadn't made plans to meet. So she lost no time in ringing Charlie. But would Sam be a true friend like Jane, uncritical, only there to help?

When Sam's call came, Emma told him about events on the Earls Court Road as quickly and as matter-of-factly as possible. There followed a long period of silence before he finally spoke, telling her in a shocked tone she might have been hurt.

"What if Jane's mother had forgotten, or garbled, the message? What then?"

His voice was controlled, but she could hear the anger coming through. And no matter how she tried to smooth things over as they talked, she felt Sam, who had snatched a few minutes from his busy day at Guy's to telephone, was furious with her for putting herself at risk. He soon rang off, telling her somewhat tersely he would be in touch. Sitting in the kitchen watching the rain, she dreads her next meeting with Sam, if indeed there will ever be one. She is probably due for another tongue-lashing.

The buzzer sounds. It is Charlie at the intercom, and she buzzes to let him in. When he arrives at the front door of the flat she takes him to the kitchen table and pours him a mug of coffee. Together they sip, looking out silently at the great grey dome of rain falling over London.

"I thought you might want to hear what happened to Mike and Uncle Scopas," he says casually, crossing his long legs and relaxing.

"Yes, I've been wondering. First of all, thanks again for appearing at the flat on Earls Court Road at that moment. I, I know I did something very foolish, going out on my own." She looks down at her hands.

"Yes, well, I wouldn't call it foolish exactly. You sized up the situation pretty well when you talked to Alexis. Sometimes, Emma, you have to commit, even if you don't know exactly what's ahead. We'd never find out anything, if we didn't. And besides, you left a clear message with an adult for another adult, a friend, who was bound to understand, to read between the lines, as it were." Charlie takes a large gulp of the coffee.

"I think you are much too hard on yourself, Emma. We captured two people who are the prime suspects because of you, didn't we?" Charlie looks at her intently. "Sam giving you a bit of a hard time over this?" he guesses shrewdly.

Emma nods, but doesn't offer to say more. Charlie resumes his account.

"Of course, I'd been outside the door of Alexis's flat for some time listening before I barged in. Scopas was all bluster, Emma. He knew better than to try anything funny in London, whatever he might undertake in the hills outside Olympia. I could tell by his tone of voice. I didn't have to see him."

"You mean you were outside Alex's flat listening?" Emma is amazed. Charlie nods.

"Keeping a low profile, of course," he amends modestly, brushing an imaginary crumb off the table. "I was hiding in that forest of mopeds and bicycles when Uncle Scopas arrived. Actually, I set out for the Earls Court Road the second Jane tipped me off. Got a terrible cramp in my legs, crouching behind all the conveyances outside Alex's flat."

Emma is silent, digesting everything Charlie has said. "How were you able to get the door open?" she finally asks, remembering how he had swanned into the room as though he lived there, without a care in the world.

"It was already open a tick with a bit of paper I wedged in when Uncle Scopas came calling. I caught the door before it locked shut." Emma looks at him, thinking, Scotland Yard is lucky indeed to have Charlie St. Cyr on their side.

"Now for the conclusion," Charlie hastens on, before she embarrasses him, gushing with praise.

"Uncle Scopas boarded a flight for Athens before the evening was underway, before you could whistle Yankee Doodle, you might say. Trip courtesy of Her Majesty's government, with escorts of course. Oh yes, he traveled in style, and a company of Greek dignitaries, policemen, met him when he set down in Athens. I say, is that airport still as cheerful as the waiting room of Pluto's Underworld? That's how I remember it."

"About as cheerful as a funeral parlor," Emma agrees, shivering. "And did you ask him about the Bassae Shepherd?"

"You know, that's a real puzzle. We grilled him over and over about the hit and run death and the chap insists that he didn't know anything about it. The funny thing is, I actually believe him. Me, old cynical Charlie. Can you credit it?" He shakes his head. "We didn't turn up a shred of information along that line of inquiry."

"So what is going to happen now?" Emma asks.

"Well, the police in Athens will certainly want him to help with their inquiries. His brother Petrus is already helping. They'll get to the bottom of the shepherd's death I feel sure."

"Well, I've got to hand it to Scotland Yard. You people really know your business." Emma looks at him with admiration. "And Mike Leonidas? What will happen to him?"

"Mike will have a little court appearance to look forward to soon," he replies. "Right now, he's released to go back to his job, on my recommendation. He'll have to explain to a judge why he nicked a suitcase at Heathrow and entered a flat in Belgravia, posing as a window cleaner, and tied up a frail little old lady. Not that Mrs. Mudge is exactly frail; at least her vocal chords are certainly working in tip-top order.

"No insurmountable difficulties loom on the horizon for Mike," Charlie continues smoothly. "A good solicitor can lead him through that court appearance blindfolded. Actually, he has one already, a cousin of mine who takes on a certain number of non-remunerative briefs." Charlie studies his fingernails.

"A cousin of yours? You picked him for Mike, didn't you?" Emma guesses as she looks into Charlie's eyes. Her mind races ahead. "Then you must believe that Mike's innocent, just as I believe it."

"I must admit, I feel a bit sorry for the poor blighter. Tossed this way and that by his father and that viper of an uncle. I do believe he's an honest chap at heart. Could do worse than fall into the clutches of that Alexis. Not a stunner for looks, but she'd see he keeps to the straight and narrow. Has a mind of her own." Deftly Charlie turns the conversation away from his good deed.

"Say, why do you think the Greeks carry that family loyalty thing to the very edge of the cliff?"

Emma laughs. It is good to laugh after all that has happened. Charlie is like a tonic for her.

"I say, Old Girl, I'm feeling a bit peckish. Truthfully, I'm limp with hunger. We're only a block away from Drones. What do you say we nosh down? I could do with a bite of their steak and kidney pudding before I get back to real work." Charlie grins engagingly.

"Yes, I'd love it." Emma suddenly feels she wants to be somewhere cheerful, someplace buzzing with people, far away from thinking of the dreary details of the case. "Let's get Jane."

"Bad luck. I've already checked. She and Mummy have made plans. Jane couldn't get loose. What about Sam?"

"He could never get away on a minute's notice," Emma says. "Besides, I'm afraid I am permanently blacklisted with him for going off on my own to play detective. You've already guessed that, haven't you? He called me yesterday He could have been in Antartica, he was so frosty after I'd told him what happened."

"Don't be too hard on yourself. He'll come around."

Dodging puddles they hurry to Charlie's unmarked car, resting of course, in a No Parking space. Soon they are relaxing in the subdued yet lively surroundings of Drones. Thoughtful lighting, delicious food, colorful quilts hanging on the walls, combine to make it one of the favorite haunts of younger Belgravia. Emma feels her natural good spirits rise.

Charlie is at his most convivial. He tells her of growing up in Wiltshire, where his father raises prize cattle on his farm and his mother grows prize delphiniums and serves as a magistrate in the county. The farm is near the picturesque village of Lacock, one of a handful of villages in England listed for historic preservation in its entirety.

"Great inn at Lacock," Charlie says. "Sign of the Angel. They make the best treacle tart anywhere in England. We'll get together with Jane and

Sam and go down sometime," he mumbles, mouth full of Drones steak and kidney pudding.

He wants to know everything about life in the United States. Do the police there fire away as often as they do on the television screen? Is that Dallas sit-com true to life? What are the mountains like, the Blue Ridge she is always going on about? Then they discuss the amulet, now turned over to the jewel experts at the BM. Are the experts edging toward the same opinion Miss Crawford has put forth, that the piece is a repro-copy of the late 1800s? No solid conclusions yet, Charlie tells her.

"What do you think of Miss Crawford?" Emma asks.

Charlie considers for a moment, fork resting on his plate. "I think she's brilliant, knows what she's talking about. I'll be surprised if she isn't right on the button. And if the amulet is nineteenth century, it could be the only existing copy of that lost original by Phidias. In other words, it would validate the theory that such a jewel actually existed."

"You're right, Charlie," Emma agrees. "I'd never thought of that."

"Much as I'd like to claim it for my own, I'm bound to tell you Jane said it first." Emma catches the respect in Charlie's voice. "That girl is going to end up lecturing, I feel it in my bones." Charlie sounds nonchalant, but Emma senses his feelings for Jane are far from indifferent.

As they are leaving Drones, Brian Gibbs enters, bringing a very pretty girl on his arm whom Emma does not know. He waves to Emma, taking note of her escort. This will get back to Sam, Emma realizes. And why not? She can't sit around moping just because Sam is displeased.

Sam calls the next day. "You were spotted at Drones having a decadent lunch with a handsome chap." His voice sounds pleasant but curious.

"Oh, yes, I was with Charlie. He was bringing me up to date on events," Emma answers lightly. "Scopas, the uncle, has been escorted back to Athens into the arms of the Athens police. Mike Leonidas is out of jail on good behavior, but he has a court appearance coming up. Charlie thinks he will be found innocent."

"Well, now, I do know all of that because I had a personal visit from Mr. Charlie St. Cyr. Came to have a word yesterday while I was setting a femur. Scotland Yard seems to have carte blanche wherever the fancy takes them! He spent a good half hour singing your praises, talking of your inspired initiative in locating Mike Leonidas. He assured me you were never in the slightest danger. He was traipsing along behind you soon after you landed at the Earls Court Road, thanks to Jane who understood your message immediately and notified him.

"In short, Charlie made me feel something of a toad, Emma, and I stand corrected. I was worried about you, that's all, thinking what might have happened. Do you understand?"

His words sound like music to her ears. "Of course, Sam. I understand."

"How about going out for an Indian tonight to celebrate the successful turn of events? We could go to Khyber Pass in Westbourne Grove. I could pick you up at seven. That is, if you want to see me."

Emma feels a leap in the region of her heart. Everything is all right again. "Yes Sam, I'd love it."

Emma's heart takes wings and she walks about the flat, peering out the wide windows of the drawing room, looking down below at the slow-moving but never ending pageant of daily life in Belgravia. A Rolls glides to the kerb and a uniformed chauffer leaps out, hurrying to open the door for a woman smothered in furs, leading a small spaniel on a leash. A flower seller offers her a sheaf of perfect roses which she pays for, handing them over to the chauffer, who steps to the door of a large mansion and presses the bell.

Emma suddenly needs to join the busy, throbbing life of the city. She puts on her raincoat and humming, walks all the way to the Victoria and Albert Museum in the rain. In spite of brimming skies, the world looks bright again. She spends the afternoon at a desk in the library writing. For the first time, she is looking forward to composing the paper for class. She will call it "The Severe Style of the Pediment Sculptures at Olympia." The saga of the amulet is finished, now she can concentrate on her studies.

EIGHT

Phaedra Arrives from Corinth

Emma and Sam walk up Sloane Street toward Knightsbridge enjoying a dry evening after a day of rain, daylight lengthening as midsummer draws closer. They cross over Hyde Park at the tip of the Serpentine, coming out of the park into the Bayswater Road. In Victorian times, the Knightsbridge side of Hyde Park was considered much more fashionable. But Emma can see no difference in beauty as she looks at the fine old houses lining Bayswater facing the park.

When they reach Westbourne Grove they turn into another largely ethnic area of London lined with busy small shops keeping late closing hours. There are many restaurants. Sam expertly guides Emma through throngs of late shoppers and diners to Khyber Pass, the Indian restaurant he likes best. Inside the motif is white, walls, ceilings, even the floors, tables covered with white cloths. Indian fabrics framed and hung as art work provide splashes of vibrant color.

Thwanging music of India plays softly in the background. Emma loves the stark decor, a foil for the spicy food. Most Indian restaurants care little about how they present themselves, she reflects. Patterned wallpaper, linoleum floor covering of a different, usually clashing, pattern, a melee of colored cloths draping the tables. By contrast Khyber is stark, cool, sparse. And the food she has heard is outstanding.

They order a lamb korma and a hot vindaloo curry with fragrant rice, *nan*, the traditional Indian bread, *bhindi*, a spicy okra dish which reminds Emma of her home in the South, and *dal*, pureed chick peas. The food arrives along with *riata*, the sauce made of cucumber, yogurt and mint to cool down the spicy food.

"I told you some time back about a paper I was being hounded to write by my registrar," Sam says as they eat.

"Yes, I remember. You said he thought you should not go to Greece and instead go up to Cambridge on your holiday and work on it. Is it that important?"

"Possibly," Sam answers thoughtfully, breaking off a corner of the *nan* and mopping up some of the korma sauce. "You see, the writer of the paper judged the winner wins a post at the best teaching hospital in Aberdeen next January."

Emma looks at him. Can he be thinking of us, wondering how I'll feel if he leaves London, wondering if Scotland would be right for us? She considers the past week which has brought them closer after the misunderstanding about the Earls Court Road, how her admiration for him has grown steadily since they met. He is unlike anyone she's ever known. Certainly he is quieter, more mature than the shadowy men of her college days.

"Sam," she says softly, "I've always been open about what I want to do after my year in London ends. I'm going to try my hardest to land a curatorial job in a museum, probably back in America. I've never pretended anything different."

"No, you haven't," he says slowly, gazing at her carefully across the table. "It's just that somehow we've grown a lot closer than just members of a London University group touring Greece together. Somewhere along the way my feelings for you have ratcheted upward several notches." He looks at her solemnly, eyes holding hers.

"And so have mine," Emma answers softly as he places his hand over hers on the white tablecloth.

"Look, neither of us believes in rushing things. Why can't we just enjoy our time together, keep to whatever career plans develop for us, and if it means I go back home, or if you go to Aberdeen, well, we'll see how being apart works. If being apart is unbearable, if our feelings are that strong for each other, we can take steps to do something about it. If not . . ." Emma shrugs.

"I try to imagine you as the wife of say a small town doctor and how you'd cope." Sam smiles ruefully as he uses a bit of *nan* to mop up the last of the vindaloo. "It's difficult for me to imagine you in a village or any small place."

"That wouldn't be impossible," she answers. "Remember I come from a very small town, a village, really. Crozet is outside Charlottesville. But I won't pretend I don't love living in London. What I have difficulty imagining is *you* living in the United States." She is rewarded by a look of surprise on Sam's face. That he hadn't considered!

Arm in arm they leave Khyber each aware that an understanding of sorts has been reached, an unspoken agreement between them. Neither will make demands of the other, not yet. And when the time comes, when they are closer, they will discuss the future, calmly and carefully.

They pass the popular Greek restaurant Mamma Moussaka from whose dim interior seeps the sound of wailing bouzouki music.

"Maybe we should have dinner here sometime, they're bound to have retsina and barbecued goat on the menu!" Sam jokes. Suddenly Emma catches sight of Alexis Sobranos coming out with a friend, a dark girl, short and attractively plump.

"Alexis," Emma calls to her. "How lovely to see you. How is Mike?"

But when Alexis recognizes her, she acknowledges Emma with a slight nod and the briefest whisper of a smile. Her eyes look unhappy, her face seems pinched. She walks away from Emma and Sam in the opposite direction, her friend trailing behind her.

"How odd," Emma exclaims, "I wonder what her problem is?"

Earlier she talked about Alexis to Sam, told him how she had helped Mike Leonidas, been a positive influence and tried to get him to go to the police. I'll go see her at the travel agency soon, Emma tells herself.

When they reach Chesham Place, Sam promises to ring Emma, "as soon as I finish the wretched paper," he mutters.

Emma tells him she will also be busy writing the paper due for her class.

"I'm going to chain myself to a desk in the library of the Victoria and Albert Museum until I finish it. You'll see."

But the following morning on an impulse, Emma decides to make her way to Charlotte Street and the Grecian Isles travel agency. She wants to chat with Alexis to find out what is wrong. Alexis should be happy that everything is working out for Mike. After all, she reasons, without Charlie's intervention, he may well have found himself on a plane bound for Athens, a prison sentence looming. The only thing hanging over his head is a court appearance, an appearance that has every indication of being 'just routine', to use Charlie's own words. Alexis is alone in the office when she arrives.

"Where's Mike?" Emma asks in surprise.

"Gone out," Alexis answers shortly. Again Emma is struck by the strained look on her face, the rude answer.

"Surely you do not mean he has left his job? Where has he gone?"

"Oh no, he is still employed here and lives over the office," she says, her voice sarcastic. "He just does not seem to find the time to put in an appearance, now that his cousin is in town, and Mr. Costas is away in Athens lining up a big tour this week." Her large brown eyes overflow and tears course down her cheeks.

"Alexis, don't be upset. What has he done?" Emma feels a pang. Has he gotten into any more trouble? "I thought things were getting better for you both, now that the amulet business is finished. Mike's uncle is in the hands of the police and can't threaten him anymore. Who is this cousin?"

"His cousin Phaedra from Corinth," Alexis answers, fighting for composure. "He's saying because she is his cousin, a second cousin," she amends angrily, "he has to show her around, go where she wants to go, do her bidding. It's that old family thing again. I'm sick of it." She shakes her head.

Emma focuses her mind on the town of Corinth. They went there, one of their first days in Greece, but only to the temple of Apollo, a temple with seven columns standing, Doric columns, if she remembers rightly. But of the city itself, only a blur remains. It was not a spot to which Maria Crawford devoted much time. Her thoughts fly back to Alex and Phaedra.

"Everything went well for a time," Alexis resumes. "He settled down, worked really hard. Mr. Costas was so pleased with him, glad he'd given Mike another chance. Then *she* shows up. Mike is weak, I tell you. He bends with the wind."

"But surely he is just being friendly to a relative. You don't think he is, well, attracted to her, do you?" Emma asks.

"Frankly I don't know what to think. Phaedra told me the family has always wanted her to marry Mike." Alexis sadly examines her blood red nails.

"And Mike, what does he say about this Phaedra?"

Alexis dabs at her eyes again. "He didn't hear her say it and I couldn't ask him, really I couldn't. He's just wishy-washy, that's what." She takes a white handkerchief out of her shoulder bag and blows her nose.

"When they are in the office, they are always talking together, and she's whispering so I can't hear, as though she's trying to upset me." Alexis sighs, spilling out her resentment. "I feel hurt and let down. I risked a lot for Mike when he needed help. He seems to have forgotten all that."

Emma sighs inwardly. Greek families and their convoluted loyalties. She will have to inform Charlie of this latest development. It appears that Mike, at the very least, is a person who cannot refuse any request from family members. Giving what words of comfort she can to Alexis, she invites her to lunch at the flat.

"Don't give up on Mike," she calls to Alexis in parting. "Remember, he's got to walk a tightrope and stay out of trouble. He can be jailed in a heartbeat if he doesn't."

"I guess that's why I'm so worried," Alexis says, frowning as she takes up her work.

~

Making her way across town on the tube toward the V. & A. library Emma glances at the headlines at the news kiosk as she comes up from the underground. BM EXPERTS BRAND SMUGGLED AMULET 'FAKE'! scream the words. She quickly buys a copy of the Evening Standard and begins to read.

"A report issued today by jewel experts at the British Museum disclosed that the supposed 5th century BC amulet smuggled in from Greece some weeks earlier is not the original. It is a copy, probably made in Naples in the 18th century by an unknown Neapolitan artisan.

"It was earlier thought the amulet, called the 'Apollo Amulet' because it portrays the figure of a Greek god in battle dress, was made by the 5th century BC sculptor Phidias, who worked on the Parthenon in Athens along with Ictinos, the architect. Ictinos was also the architect of the remote Temple of Apollo, Bassae, where the lost amulet from antiquity was believed to have originated and was thought to be the work of Phidias.

"Even so," the article continues, "Scotland Yard is treating the theft as extremely serious. The amulet is believed to have been smuggled into Heathrow in an unsuspecting passenger's luggage. The identity of the passenger has not been revealed.

"At least one Greek national, Scopas Leonidas, has been apprehended and deported. There are reported to be others helping police with their inquiries. Leonidas is known to have connections with members of a radical Greek-Cypriot organization.

"Leading jewel experts examined the amulet (drawing seen at right) at some length and have just released their findings. Those signing the report include . . ." Emma's eyes slide over the lengthy list of experts. So Miss

Crawford and Jane were correct. This really seems to put the matter to rest, she thinks, mounting the steps of the Victoria and Albert Museum, a South Kensington landmark. She goes to the library on the first floor.

Once seated at a comfortable table in the library, she takes out her notes and begins working. But her eyes stray to the drawing of the amulet in the newspaper. After an hour, she stretches and decides to make her way to the museum tearoom on the ground floor. She feels a crick coming on in her neck. Maybe a cup of tea will help.

She passes the huge Plaster Cast Court on the way, a cavernous room filled with plaster casts: building facades, sculptures, columns from famous monuments all over the world. Glancing in, Emma marvels at the Victorian mind, always eager to collect examples of the world's finest specimens in whatever category, from butterflies to battlements. That's what makes London's many museums and galleries so rich and unique, she muses, with the plaster cast room leading the bizarre category. The room has an incredibly high ceiling to accommodate soaring columns and facades.

Pausing to glance around, she notices a young couple, deep in conversation, standing close to a Greek *stele*, a funerary monument, of a mourning woman.

With a start she recognizes Mike Leonidas. Emma feels certain the woman with him must be his cousin, Phaedra Patakis. The girl is pretty in a sharp, brittle sort of way, her coarse, dark hair bleached with blonde streaks, dark roots showing. The eyes however, are startlingly beautiful, deep blue, fringed by the blackest of lashes, her lips full, pouting. She is thin and small, only a bit over five feet tall, exuding a confidence, a presence Emma notes instantly. Clearly someone like Mike is putty in her hands. No wonder Alexis is worried.

She hears them speaking Greek as she edges closer, lurking behind a replica of Trajan's Column in Rome, which has been cast in two parts, enabling it to fit into the court. What can they be talking about? It doesn't sound like light-hearted banter between sweethearts. Emma is frustrated by her inability to understand.

Suddenly they move briskly toward the exit. She follows as close as she dares. They make their way back to the floor from which Emma has come, sailing past the library entrance, entering a section of the museum set aside for the display of precious jewels.

Emma follows at a discreet distance. When they enter the jewel gallery turnstiles, she waits briefly, then follows. Emma can see where they are standing, peering intently into the glass case. She marks the location of the case in her mind and moves along. She is afraid she will be discovered, but she need not have worried. Mike is completely absorbed, and Phaedra gives her no more than an unseeing, dismissive glance. The couple examines the contents of the one case carefully and then rapidly leave the jewel galleries.

Emma hurries to the spot where the couple were standing. It contains small, Greek motif brooches, bracelets, a few amulets. Emma's eyes fall on a familiar piece, an exact replica of the Apollo Amulet. So that's what they've been looking at with such intensity! It appears to be exactly the same as the one examined by the experts. Only this amulet is displayed in the Victoria and Albert Museum! A small card beneath reads 'Neapolitan, 18th century. Given to the museum in 1875 by Miss Emily Butterworth. Copy of an original, now lost, by the Greek sculptor, Phidias, 5th century BC'.

Emma is dumbfounded. If the BM experts had bothered to look, presumably they could have got their information from the V. & A! The jealousy of art historians! Emma knows they will do anything to keep from giving credit to a rival, or a rival institution. But were any of them even aware of this second amulet? Emma mulls this over in her mind as she looks at the amulet long and hard.

Now why are that pair so interested in this replica of the amulet? You would think Mike might wish to put it all behind him as quickly as possible. Can he possibly be plotting something with Phaedra? Hurriedly Emma leaves the jewel galleries, gathers up her papers from the library and heads for telephones in the foyer of the museum. Frowning, she dials Charlie's number.

Temple of Apollo, Corinth

Later in the week, Emma and Alexis Sobranos are enjoying a salad lunch in the Belfrage yellow and white kitchen. Alexis seemed happier, more relaxed than at their last meeting. She reports Mike seems to have come to his senses and isn't seeing much of Phaedra, at least not during working hours. Phaedra is still in London, however, and feels free to drop by the agency whenever she wishes.

Alexis makes a face, "I wouldn't care if she never came in again."

Alexis tells Emma that Phaedra rents a stall at Portobello Road antique market on Saturdays. When she has sold all her jewelry, she buys supplies, then returns to her home in Corinth. It is a schedule she repeats several times a year.

Emma asks Alexis what Mike had said to her, if anything, about the Apollo Amulet.

"Not much, really," she replies. She shrugs, "He read in the paper about it being a fake, a copy, made in the 18th century. As I recall he said something about how much of a fuss over something that turned out to be worthless."

Clearly Alexis is doing her best to keep Mike out of any more family entanglements. And Emma knows Charlie also is keeping close tabs on Mike. He has reported to Emma that Mike is being careful to keep all of his actions open and above board. He has too much to lose by getting into trouble. One transgression and poof! He could be deported in a twinkling; then the Athens police would deal swiftly with the problem of Michael Leonidas. So why were he and his cousin looking at the amulet in the jewel gallery of the Victoria and Albert Museum? Probably for no serious reason, Charlie has said.

But just to be on the safe side, Charlie has told her, Officer Margery Parsley has a new assignment. She is now working undercover as a museum guard at the V.& A., in the jewel galleries. And sure enough, Emma spots her by accident one afternoon when she goes in for another look at the amulet.

Margery's green eyes give a flicker of recognition when she sees Emma, but she says nothing. Surely Charlie doesn't think anyone will be foolish enough to try to heist a jewel out of that gallery, Emma reasons. But he isn't taking any chances! Emma reports this to Alexis, and senses Alexis wishes to forget about amulets.

They finish lunch and Alex returns to Charlotte Street and her desk at the travel agency. As they part, Emma begs her to keep up her courage. Things are going to turn out all right for Mike, for both of them, she feels certain. She asks Alex to promise to keep her posted of any new developments.

Tidying the kitchen, Emma lets her thoughts wander. So what of the amulet at the V.&A.? How does it fit into the puzzle? Surely the Greek-Cypriot radicals won't try to steal it. Even they can surely see it is hopeless, and not worth a fraction of what the original would have brought. A much more credible possibility is that Phaedra, if she is planning anything at all, would like to make copies of the amulet to sell at her jewelry stall. It is an attractive idea, one that a skilled jeweler might accomplish, if he or she has the expertise needed to model and carve. But Emma wonders if Phaedra has that skill.

~

Shortly after Alexis returns from lunch with Emma, Mike takes his lunch break from the travel agency. He has hardly cleared the premises before he is unexpectedly joined by a jovial Charlie St. Cyr. Mike's features droop. He doesn't dislike Charlie, but his surprise appearance makes him wary.

"Hello, Mike, I thought we might have a bite of lunch together. Is the Kebab Palace here okay?" Mike nods glumly with an obvious lack of enthusiasm. Charlie seems not to notice. They go in and find a table.

"Look," Mike speaks up. "I'm keeping my hands clean. I go to my job. I stay out of trouble. I'm certainly not thinking of chucking everything and scarpering. Why can't you leave me alone?"

"Because," Charlie answers, his voice steely, "we've discovered another amulet. This one's at the V.& A. and some mighty interesting people have been in there studying it. Why?"

His eyes bore into Mike. Mike suddenly feels his hands go clammy. Scotland Yard has the instincts of a pack of bloodhounds. A fellow can't breathe without attracting their attention. Somebody has seen him there with Phaedra. Not that it amounts to anything. He just doesn't like everybody being so nosy about his life.

"Who is she, Mike? What's her business?" Charlie waits.

I'm sure you can tell me, Mike thinks, but doesn't dare say so aloud.

"Her name is Phaedra Patakis. She comes from Corinth. She is a cousin of mine. She showed up a while back. Told me she had heard about another amulet and wondered if it was like the first. That seems harmless enough."

"What's her occupation, Mike?" Charlie's friendly blue eyes narrow and his voice is clipped.

"She's a jeweler, just costume stuff. Mostly beads and glass. Cheap, nothing pricey. But surely you can understand how she wanted to see the amulet?"

"You certain there's not another plan afoot to nick that amulet for the folks back home?" Charlie speaks in a low voice, almost a whisper.

Mike's eyes widen with fear. "Santa Maria! Do you think I'm looney enough to try that? Only an idiot would even think about lifting something from the Victoria and Albert Museum! It's wired from top to bottom. There are gates that fly up if you press a button. The Silver Vaults can't hold a candle as far as security goes, in my opinion."

Charlie allows himself a small smile. Officer Parsley has already brought him into the picture on security. He knows it is tight as, well, like Mike says, The Silver Vaults, overflowing with gleaming silver objects.

"So this cousin of yours. Phaedra. Her trip is just a pleasure jaunt?"

"No." Mike keeps his voice even. "I told you. She is a jewelry maker. She rents a stall on the Portobello Road on Saturdays. When she sells everything, she buys jewelry supplies and flies back home. She makes enough to pay her airfare and to buy supplies to make the jewelry. Not much more. But she likes coming to London."

"Declares everything at customs I suppose?" Charlie asks innocently, looking up at the ceiling of the café.

Mike keeps silent. The look on his face is one of hopeless resignation. It is surely another threat, subtle of course, to let him know that Charlie is watching his every move.

"Oh, well," Charlie brightens suddenly. "If she forgets to declare every little thing, she's no worse than ninety per cent of the British traveling public." Charlie rolls his eyes innocently, rising from the table. "You'll keep in touch, won't you, Mike?" he drawls, leaving his money on the table and walking from the cafe.

Mike looks down at his *souvlaki* but he no longer has an appetite. How could he have gotten his life in such a mess? He doesn't care for Phaedra that much. She is so bossy! But he must be friendly with her, she is his cousin. She is family. He knows Alexis is sore at him because of her. Suddenly disgusted, he throws down his napkin, pays his bill.

As he walks back to work, he asks himself, can she be up to anything devious? Is there a motive she hasn't revealed to him? Is there something going on that makes Scotland Yard suspicious? He wonders, recalls that his cousin is devious and tricky, not honest and straight like Alexis. He begins wondering if Phaedra is plotting something underhand.

~

Emma and Jane, ensconced in the kitchen of the Belfrage flat are cooking, a special dinner for Sam and Charlie. It is to be a Greek meal, and vestiges of the ingredients dot the countertops of the ample, well-equipped kitchen. A variety of salad greens and small Dutch tomatoes lie in the sink, ready to be washed. A large wedge of goat cheese and a carton of dark Greek olives swimming in brine wait in deli cartons. Moussaka will be the main course. A Greek salad, then yogurt drizzled with honey for dessert will complete the meal.

Emma bends over the minced lamb, carefully adding spices to the browning pan. "I hope they appreciate this dinner. I never knew moussaka could be so much work. I guess I should have realized, there are so many ingredients."

Jane patiently pats draining eggplant slices with a paper towel. They will go into the browning pan after the lamb has been removed.

"The cookbook says when you have everything assembled and layered into the casserole, then you cover it with a topping of mashed potatoes. Is there a pastry tube anywhere? If you have one, we could pipe the potatoes on. Then it would really look professional." Jane pushes a lock of hair away from her forehead. Emma realizes that Jane knows her way around the kitchen very well. Probably her father taught her. She has trouble picturing Felicity Hale, hot and flushed, boning a roast, or making a hollandaise sauce. Emma shakes her head.

"I'm pretty sure there isn't one. We'll just have to make-do with spooning on the potatoes. We really deserve a Cordon Bleu toque after struggling with this dish."

Emma sighs. Cooking is not her favorite pastime. She doesn't enjoy it nearly as much as Jane, who delights in concocting new dishes, especially desserts.

"Do you think perhaps we should serve some *baklava* for dessert?" Jane asks. "Yogurt and honey might not be enough. Men have huge appetites, you know."

"You mean make it *now*, at this stage?" Emma's voice registers dismay.

"No, silly. Harrods pastry shop makes the best *baklava* in London. Why don't I pop over and get some?" Jane unties her apron strings and prepares to hurry off to Harrods in Basil Street, just a few blocks away from the Belfrage flat.

Emma sets the large pan of moussaka into the oven and closes the door with a sigh of relief. She sets the table, adding a centerpiece of summer flowers purchased from Harry, the corner flower vendor who has become her friend. Harry, whose son is a student at Cambridge, began selling vegetables from a barrow in the East End market; now he owns a flower stall in upscale Belgravia in the heart of London.

Once Emma, looking down on Chesham Place from her window, saw Harry chase down a thief. He nabbed him beside a Number twenty two double decker bus and held him until a Bobby arrived with handcuffs.

She steps back to admire the effect of her efforts in the dining room. The high ceilings of the room with its lovely moldings looks inviting. The antique walnut table is bare, in the English style, its polished surface reflecting gleaming crystal and silver. Not too bad, Emma thinks, setting out a heavily chased silver tray for serving the *baklava*.

Sam and Charlie arrive on the stroke of seven, bearing more flowers and a bottle of wine. Smart in dark jackets and striped ties, they sniff with appreciation the delicious aromas seeping over the flat from the direction of the kitchen. Jane lights the tall tapers and invites everyone to sit down.

The big casserole of steaming moussaka is carried in to the sideboard along with the wooden bowl of Greek salad, bread and butter. They serve themselves buffet style. Sam and Charlie begin to eat, visibly impressed with the girls' efforts. Jane and Emma smile at each other. A success. Charlie proposes a toast after the main course.

"First to the Queen, then to the cooks." They stand around the table and raise their glasses. Emma smiles at Jane and Charlie, then at Sam. It will be difficult, leaving London which she loves, and all of the friends she has made.

After dinner, they discuss the mysterious woman, Phaedra. Is she just an innocent visitor as it seems, or is she on a more dangerous, secret mission?

"From the brief sightings I got in the V. and A., she looks like the kind of woman who could cause lots of trouble," Emma says.

"I can vouch for one thing," Charlie tells them. "Those jewel galleries at the V.& A. are tamper-proof."

"I think she's just here to sell her wares, make a little money, and then go back home," Jane says. "Look, it's a vacation for her. That's all."

Emma isn't so sure. "She seems to be such an intense person. I feel certain she's got some hidden motive we know nothing about."

"Well," Sam says smiling, "Just be sure you are careful when you go sleuthing."

"That's like asking Emma to stop breathing, Old Chap," Charlie says. "Of course Phaedra may be planning to copy the amulet, make a reproduction of it she can sell."

"Ah, but that depends on how good a jeweler she really is," Sam adds. "Modeling and carving are of a pretty high standard on that piece. Copying masterpieces has an honorable history of a thousand years," he reflects. "But you've got to have the skills to do it well."

"And Mike Leonidas?" Emma asks.

"He's not involved. I would bet on it." Charlie says flatly. He's as much in the dark as we are about his cousin. At least, that's what I believe. He knows we'll come down hard on him if he puts one foot out of line. I've made that blindingly clear."

"And so the second amulet at the Victoria and Albert is worth no more than the first?" Sam inquires. Jane nods.

"No more than the one smuggled in. They were probably turned out by the same artisan at the same time. Wouldn't it be fun to know how one was bought by or given to Miss Emily Butterworth in London 'way back in the last century, and how the other found its way to the area near Bassae? Now there's a tale." Jane's grey eyes sparkle with excitement.

The dinner turns out to be something of a celebration. Sam has mailed off his paper to Aberdeen. Emma and Jane have completed their essays and submitted them to Miss Crawford's scrutiny.

"What's your reason for celebrating, Charlie?" Emma grins at him.

"I know. Charlie's birthday is coming Sunday," Jane smile lights up the room, making the candlelight seem pale. "So tonight's dinner is an early birthday celebration," she adds.

"I didn't think anyone knew," he mutters, but looks pleased.

Charlie and Sam leave Chesham Place around eleven, but it is after midnight when Jane and Emma finish tidying up, returning the Belfrage kitchen to pristine order. The washing up leaves their hands wrinkled as prunes. They realize they have succeeded brilliantly with dinner as they turn out the lights, hang up the last dish towel, and leave the kitchen.

"I hope they don't think our dinner invitations will become a regular thing," says Emma, looking at her water-wrinkled fingers. "Cooking is so much work."

"But Emma, think of all the fun it will be when we settle down to a place of our own somewhere and can have our friends as dinner guests to our own place! There are heaps of things one can serve instead of what we labored over tonight! Mummy always says roast beef is everybody's favorite, and terribly easy when the vegetables go in the pan to roast along with the meat. Think of the lovely parsnips, carrots and leeks. Even potatoes in their jackets are easier than mashed potatoes, unless they're twice baked," she adds, hoping to win Emma over. Emma, while somewhat thoughtful, isn't completely convinced, although she admits entertaining in one's own flat would be fun.

"And so much cheaper than trekking to a pricey restaurant," Jane adds with a smile, turning into the guest bedroom. "Goodnight, Emma. Don't wake me 'til noon!"

NINE

A Guiness Party at the Man in the Moon Pub on Portobello Road

The Saturday before Charlie's birthday, Emma and Jane make a trip to Portobello Road so Jane can shop for a birthday present for Charlie. They climb aboard a Number Fifty Two double decker bus at Knightsbridge, bound for Notting Hill.

The magic of green leaves and flower blossoms, summer, in all of its promise, has burst upon London, filling the air, bringing clouds like plump white cushions floating overhead, a sky as fine as the blue silk of a nymph's drapery in a Tiepolo ceiling, Emma imagines. Sunshine sparkles on windows, dappling the streets beneath giant plane trees, turning into mottled, decorative shadows suitable for a park scene by Bonnard.

As the bus meanders along Emma tries to fit bits of the amulet puzzle together in her mind. She still has no explanation, no real one, for Phaedra's sudden arrival from Greece. Her manipulative cunning, however, disturbs Emma, who fears unknown motives. Motives that go beyond running a small, insignificant jewelry stall. She turns her thoughts to the business of the morning, finding a suitable gift for Jane to present to Charlie for his birthday.

They walk from the bus stop a few blocks to Portobello Road, vibrating with the sights and sounds of an antique market every Saturday morning, transforming the street into a pedestrian walkway. Emma keeps an eye out for a possible gift for her parents now that her time in London is growing short. But finding Charlie's gift is the main focus of the expedition. Jane has her heart set on an old piece of jewelry, a stick pin, perhaps. She thinks this would mean more to Charlie than, say, an ordinary tie from Harrods.

"A tie is what Mummy suggested," she murmurs as they jostle along with the crowd, peering at the antique objects on tables laid out before them. "But I think Charlie would prefer something more personal, not necessarily expensive, just a token. I wish I could find a small stick pin or cuff links engraved with small swans. The swan is on his family's crest, St. Cyr being the French spelling of the word of course. That would be perfect."

Jane recently spent a weekend in Wiltshire with Charlie and his parents on their farm. Emma realizes she and Charlie have become an item.

They amble down one side of Portobello Road and prepare to reverse and return to their starting point by inspecting the other side when Emma spots a beautiful pair of old Sheffield silver candlesticks. Victorian, silver with a copper underlay beginning to show through in a few places, gives a wonderful patina to the surface. The intricate tracery of the pieces is unique. Emma purchases them at once, convinced they are a treasure, and a bargain at twenty pounds.

"Here's a man's mourning ring," she notices, bending over the next stall as they move along. "Look: the brown hair has been woven into a tiny braid around the blue stone, all covered in glass. Would Charlie like something like that?"

Jane looks doubtful. "I don't think so, Emma. After all, I'm not dead."

They pause at a stall topped by a canvas umbrella stamped with the words "Spratt, Daniel & Son, Bishopsgate, E.C.1." The stall sparkles with appealing Victorian jewelry and charming objects of *virtu*. Emma's eyes catch the glimmer of a metal, similar to gold. It is a seal, beautifully worked, with a ring on one end so it can be attached to a watch chain. The seal itself is onyx with an engraving. Upon closer inspection, Emma discovers a tiny swan.

"Jane, look what I've found."

"Why it's a swan. How lovely." Jane's face lights up.

"Why yer two, yer've found my Pinchbeck seal, yer 'ave."

Emma, startled, looks quickly to see if Mrs. Mudge is behind her. But it is a short, jovial man, cheeks criss-crossed with wrinkles, nodding at them in a friendly way. A Cockney from the East End Emma notes, reading the sign on the umbrella for the second time.

"I sez when I packed up this mornin: 'Mother,' I sez, 'I've got a feelin' someun's goin' to buy me seal today,' I did." The dapper little man grins. "Know what kind of metal this is? It's called Pinchbeck, a metal alloy a watchmaker called Pinchbeck discovered in the early 1700s. An alloy it were, of copper and zinc. It made a good, cheap substitute for gold, it did." His face puckers as a huge smile breaks over his face. He eyes the seal fondly.

"It were a howlin' success, it were, that alloy. Cost a lot less than gold, kept its color and didn't turn green, no siree. Trouble was, 'e died, Mr. Pinchbeck did, and took the secret formula with 'em. No more Pinchbeck made today! Makes it more precious, dun' it?"

Jane has not removed her eyes from the seal. "How much is it?" she whispers.

"Fifteen pounds, but fourteen to yer, Luv," says Mr. Spratt. "I see yer not one to 'aggle like most is. Fourteen British pounds."

"I'll take it," Jane breathes with rapture. "It will be perfect."

Emma meanwhile has been inspecting the adjacent stall which is unattended.

"Whose stall is this, Mr. Spratt?" she asks, bending over a meager assortment of pins, earrings and bracelets displayed on a not-too-clean scarf of some cheap material of a garish print. Crudely fashioned owls, helmets and Grecian keys comprise the jewelry motifs.

"Oh, that one," Mr. Spratt scoffs. "'Er's never here. Asks me to keep a lookout, dun' 'er? What sort of a merchant is that, I ask yer. Just now 'er ran off down to the pub with another stranger, a furriner, judgin' from his looks. Said 'er'd be back in a tick, didn't 'er?" He shakes his head dismissively. "Nobody buys 'er stuff, anyroad."

"Which pub is that, Mr. Spratt?" Emma asks quickly.

"Why The Man in the Moon, right over yonder. Yer kin see the sign."

And indeed she can, looking in the direction to which he points. She takes off at a run, calling to Jane to follow her. Quickly Jane hands over fourteen pounds, thanks Mr. Spratt prettily as she accepts the seal, neatly wrapped in brown paper, and hurries after Emma.

What is going on? Emma doesn't usually behave like this. Loyally, Jane hurries as fast as she can to catch up, wondering what Emma can be thinking.

"Emma," she gasps as they reach the pub entrance together, breathing heavily from their efforts. "Have you gone bonkers? What on earth has possessed you?"

"Quick Jane, I'll explain later. Come with me, and quietly now." They slip into the pub.

This pub wouldn't win the Best of Britain pub competition, Emma thinks, noting the gloomy, smoke-filled atmosphere. But as her eyes become more accustomed to the darkness, she spots the bleached-blond, streaked hair of

Phaedra Patakis in a distant booth. She gives silent thanks that she was right in her hunch. Phaedra's stall *is* next to Mr. Spratt! And Emma knows she is unknown to Phaedra, except for that haughty glance her way in the Victoria and Albert Museum, which she is sure Phaedra has forgotten. She hopes Mike Leonidas will not see her, if in fact he proves to be her companion.

Emma leads Jane quietly to an empty booth behind the couple. Fortuitously the booths have high wooden backs and this one has a broken slat offering a generous peep hole into the next booth. They will be able to listen, see a little and not be observed. Emma sees that Phaedra's companion is not Mike after all. He is a man Emma has never seen before. Paunchy, wearing a shiny suit of some inferior grade of silk and a loud, insistent tie, the man's hair is thinning rapidly on top. His eyes are small, ferret eyes, set close to a hawk-like nose standing out in a puffy face.

They are speaking English. A discussion of money is in progress. "Seven fifty?" Was that what she'd heard? Seven hundred fifty pounds no doubt, but for what? Emma presses her ear closer to the crack in the booth.

"Of course I can't give you any documentation!" Phaedra's voice is scornful. "You're not on Regent's Street, buying from Garrards, the Queen's jeweler!" She puffs away confidently on her gasper. She really is amazing, thinks Emma. What assurance she has, what a nerve.

"Then I will pay in lira," growls the man, hard-faced and menacing.

Italian lira, Emma acknowledges to herself. The man must be Italian. A quick vignette flashes before her of this tatty figure as a young man, engaging in petty theft on the mean streets of Naples. And now, at last, he has reached the big time.

"Oh no you don't!" Phaedra counters instantly. "Only English pounds. Only a fool would take lira."

She doesn't seem to be worried a bit that he really means it, Emma thinks, marveling at the woman's boldness as she continues to peer through the crack in the booth.

"All right, pounds then. I've brought the money, "he growls. His voice holds the promise of capitulation. Phaedra continues to puff away in triumph.

"Let's see your money," she says. There is a click and his briefcase on the table flies open, exposing rows of stacked bills.

This is a lot more than seven hundred fifty pounds, Emma realizes, pressing Jane's arm with a warning to keep quiet as Jane sees the case full of money and gives a tiny gasp.

Emma whispers in Jane's ear, "Go call Charlie, Jane! Phone him and get him here quick as you can!"

Whatever it is Phaedra is selling, it is bound to be illegal. Emma dares not let herself dream that it might be the original amulet. The man is speaking again. Emma leans as close as possible to the crack, determined not to miss one word.

"Before I give you the case with the money, I want to look at it again." The man's voice sounds onerous.

"Very well," Phaedra agrees, taking a dingy handkerchief out of her pocket and handing it to him. He unfolds it slowly, keeping his eyes on Phaedra, and lays the object on the table between them.

"I can assure you it's the real one. This one is different from those two later ones they've been writing about in all of the papers. Any collector with sense would be wild to get his hands on this." Phaedra's voice is calm now, her look one of nonchalance.

What cool, Emma thinks. Jane slips noiselessly back into the booth nodding. Charlie is on his way. Emma's rampaging stomach relaxes a bit as she strains to see what the merchandise looks like.

Her eyes make contact with the small object lying on the table. Both Phaedra and the man are hunched over it, heads together. Its color is like ivory, old ivory. It is the figure of the god Apollo, deeply carved and faintly dark. It looks extremely old. The real thing? Has Phaedra somehow managed to get her hands on the real thing? The one by Phidias? Hope springs up in Emma's heart.

Emma knows Phaedra mustn't be allowed to get away with it. But Emma realizes she and Jane will be no match for the pair in a confrontation. The man and woman are tough, operating outside the law. She and Jane must stage a delaying action of some kind. to hold them until Charlie comes. Emma's mind races as the two continue to study the amulet, talking in low tones.

"Jane," Emma's whisper is urgent. "Go to the bar and get two pitchers of beer. Please! And hurry!"

Poor Emma, thinks Jane, wondering if Emma's brain has snapped under the strain. Something is drastically wrong with her. Neither of them can bear the smell of beer, never mind the taste. But, loyal to her friend, she slips away obediently and approaches the bar, ordering two pitchers.

"What kind of beer do you want, Miss?" The bartender is polite.

Jane thinks wildly. Can she recall the name of any brand of beer?

"Guiness!" she cries triumphantly, causing several people at the bar to turn and look disapprovingly in her direction. Mortified, she pays quickly and grasps the tray with the pitchers and glasses, struggling to carry it back to the booth.

"Will that be all, Miss?" the bartender asks after her.

"Oh yes, please," Jane answers, then thinks, he must think I'm a complete fool. "I'll be back for more when we need it."

And she hurries away leaving the bartender looking faintly puzzled. She hadn't looked like a guzzler at all to him, but he knows from experience, they come in all shapes and sizes. Phaedra and her companion are still gazing at the amulet nestled in the handkerchief when she returns. Emma puts a finger to her lips.

Emma mind is jerking forward like a runaway horse, wondering how the amulet has found its way into Phaedra's hands, but never mind, she has a hunch it is the real thing. Emma is sure of it, as sure as she is that the two examples she has seen earlier are copies. Quietly she whispers to Jane. Slowly they stand up in the high-backed booth. The couple is still leaning over, gazing fixedly at the object on the table.

"All right. You've gawked enough, let's get out of here. I've got a plane to catch," Phaedra says, her rasping voice triumphant. She and her companion, are unaware of the two figures looming over them.

But before the man folds up the handkerchief and pockets the amulet and before Phaedra snaps shut the briefcase, Emma tips her pitcher and begins pouring a thin stream of beer over the couple, the briefcase, the amulet. She is methodical in her movements.

"What the hell?" shouts the man as he sees dark stains appearing on his suit. "What is going on?"

"What idiot is doing this?" rages Phaedra, snarling. She digs at her eyes with her fists. The stream of beer trickles on her hair and directly into her eyes, blinding her. But Emma keeps on pouring. The open case becomes a lake on which pound notes of large denomination float; the handkerchief, a nest for the amulet, becomes a wet shroud smelling strongly of Guiness. Jane, prolonging the delaying action, lifts the second pitcher higher sending another deluge on the hapless couple, causing Phaedra to scream.

The bartender and several patrons move quickly toward the disturbance. Just when Emma fears she and Jane have become the villains and the guilty pair will escape, sodden but scot-free, Officer Margery Parsley, followed by a Bobby of exceptional size and muscle, bursts into the Man in the Moon pub.

"Back here, Margery!" cries Emma. "Here they are, with a case of money and the original Apollo Amulet between them! There it is, on that handkerchief soaked with all the Guiness."

Her voice sounds on the edge of hysteria, and blessed relief. The Bobby quickly sizes up the scene, grabs Phaedra and her companion by the arm as Officer Parsley pockets the amulet for safekeeping, at the same time assuring the knot of patrons clustering around that the excitement is over, they can return to their seats.

Jane has stopped pouring but her arm holding the nearly empty pitcher aloft is frozen, like Lady Liberty holding her torch, Emma thinks wildly as she turns her eyes back to the pair, dripping with the remains of the beer and continuing to mouth curses. That is how Charlie sees them as he hurries into the Man in the Moon.

A soaking, sputtering Phaedra rants against tyranny and injustice as she and her partner, who threatens them repeatedly using highly creative expletives in Italian, are led out in handcuffs by the Bobby while Charlie accepts the amulet from Officer Parsley, places a snowy handkerchief over it and secures it in his breast pocket. Officer Parsley neatly dumps the beer out of the briefcase and snaps it shut.

"Whew! You girls stink to high heaven," Charlie says, smothering a chuckle. "Whatever made you decide to drown the pair? Strictly speaking, that wasn't necessary. Are you all right?" Dismayed, Emma surveys the mess she and Jane have made.

"Oh dear. It was the only way I could think of to hold them here. In a tussle I knew Jane and I couldn't win. I didn't want any violence. And I was so afraid they would get away before you arrived. We heard Phaedra tell the man she had a plane to catch."

"But Charlie, listen!" Jane speaks up. "That isn't the amulet from the V. & A. you've got. It's the real one, by Phidias. Honest to goodness, I'd bet my life on it."

But Charlie has his hands full at the moment, placating the bartender, assuring him the two women have acted responsibly in helping bring two dangerous criminals to justice.

"It's all right, Mate," says the bartender as he is brought into the picture, seeing that a bit of mopping up is all needed to put things right.

"They did their job pretty well by half." He looks admiringly at Emma and Jane. "Never took them for drinkers, I sure didn't."

Charlie hurries off to catch up with Officer Parsley and the captives. Explanations will have to wait. He promises Jane and Emma to be in touch as soon as he can.

~

Sunday afternoon, the day after the Guiness Party, as Jane has dubbed it, on Portobello Road, Jane and Emma enter the imposing doorway of Brown's

Hotel in Picadilly. They have been invited to attend what they suppose will be tea on Charlie's birthday. In her pocket Jane clutches the seal, still wrapped in Mr. Spratt's brown paper. All traces of Guinness have been shampooed out of their hair. Emma still imagines however, she smells the taint of beer even after several showers.

"Miss Darling? Miss Hale? Mr. St. Cyr expects you in the Regent's Room. This way."

The attendant, ancient like most of the retainers at Brown's, consults a list then shuffles along before them in a sprightly manner, leading them down a corridor to a room off the main dining area.

Emma's blue eyes register winking crystal chandeliers, oak paneling warm with age, faded yet distinguished draperies surely designed by Geoffrey Bennison in the 1920s, a high molded ceiling in the Adam style and several gilded mirrors reflecting soft lights from sconces set into the walls. The sinking feel of old Persian carpet underfoot adds to the aura of faded elegance. Several people whom she does not know already have arrived and she realizes at once that this gathering has little to do with Charlie's birthday.

Next her eyes fasten on Sam, Miss Crawford, Lance and Fiona Fenway, gathered in a corner of the room, talking animatedly. They cluster around Charlie who hurries forward when he sees Jane and Emma.

"Emma, Jane. I am delighted you are here." He guides them across the room.

"May I present Professor Peter Martin of the British Museum and Sir Lionel Latching of the Victoria and Albert. Miss Darling and Miss Hale. Do take seats now, everyone," Charlie urges.

The gathering proceeds to the circle of chairs placed around a large table. Emma finds herself sitting between Sam and Sir Lionel. Jane is beside Charlie, with Lance Fenway on her left. Miss Crawford is seated next to Professor Martin of the BM.

"I believe you may have guessed, some of you at any rate, why I have interrupted your Sunday afternoon leisure to invite you here. Nothing short of important news would compel me to do this. Scotland Yard is now in possession of what we believe to be a significant work of art, the original Amulet of Apollo." There is a slight emphasis on the word 'original.'

"All preliminary indications," Charlie continues, "point to the certainty that this amulet was made by the Greek sculptor Phidias in the fifth century BC."

"Of course," he goes on, "this assessment will need more fine tuning, but Professor Martin, Miss Crawford and Sir Lionel all of whom have examined the amulet, concur in first opinions that the work is indeed authentic." A collective gasp, followed by enthusiastic applause, breaks out.

"Scotland Yard," Charlie resumes, "is holding in custody a Greek national, Phaedra Patakis, who has related the most amazing story of theft, deception and ultimately murder. She was arrested yesterday with the amulet in her possession and is now helping police with their inquiries."

Emma rolls her eyes at Jane. The idea of Phaedra aiding the police! Can it even be imagined? But, in police parlance, she knows that is the standard phrase used in England.

"Another person, an Italian national," Charlie continues, "has been arrested for trying to purchase stolen property. He is a notorious, well-known dealer in stolen art and is wanted for art theft in a dozen countries. His name is Roberto Gubbio. There has been little time to inform you as the pair was apprehended only yesterday afternoon. That is why I asked you all to meet here, so I can tell the whole story once and only once, and we can have a nice cup of tea while you are listening."

At this point Charlie smiles, signaling the waiters who are standing by with steaming tea pots. They begin to pour the tea. Only in England, Emma thinks, as she hides a smile in her napkin while Charlie demolishes a tiny cucumber sandwich and takes a sip of tea.

"Several months ago," he begins, "the woman in custody, Phaedra Patakis of Corinth, saw an unusual piece of jewelry in a stall on the Portobello Road where she herself sells the crude pieces of jewelry she makes at her home in Greece. When she completes a supply, she brings her wares to London for sale, returning to Greece after she has purchased more jewelry supplies with her profits.

"It was on one of these trips that she saw the amulet which we all have come to know as the Apollo Amulet. She recognized what she saw because she had seen an identical piece in the Victoria and Albert Museum in South Kensington." Here a nod from Sir Lionel.

"The amulet she saw dated from the 18th century. Phaedra was able to wheedle it for a few pounds from the inexperienced dealer at Portobello Road, who did not realize its worth. She took it home to Greece. She intended to sell it at a profit somewhere, she was not sure where at that point. She made inquiries, learning that there were stories of a much older Amulet of Apollo, a legend really, a piece made by Phidias in the 5th century BC, but that piece was now lost.

"Meanwhile, some cousins of her mother belonging to a radical Greek-Cypriot group had heard of the legendary amulet which supposedly was secreted somewhere in the hills near the Temple of Bassae.

"They had been tracking the lonely shepherd rumored to be the keeper of the amulet, trying to discover where it was hidden. This man, some of you knew him as The Bassae Shepherd, was George Soutakis, a virtual hermit with no surviving family. Many people thought he was crazy." Here Charlie pauses for reflection, taking more tea.

"But George Soutakis was not crazy. He was a highly intelligent man with a strong sense of patriotism and a spotless character. Living alone, he had grown into something of an eccentric, but he certainly possessed all his faculties. The thieves followed him for weeks. Finally they were rewarded. Unwittingly, he led them to the amulet, hidden in a cave high in the hills near Bassae. When he departed the site, they lost no time in stealing it.

"Of course they wanted to raise money from the sale of the piece for their political cause. In what seemed to them a logical move, the thieves took the amulet to a relative, a maker of jewelry, for evaluation. Perhaps she would know who could sell it for them. Imagine Phaedra Patakis's surprise when they appeared, bearing the 5th century BC original of the copied piece she recently had picked up for a song from a stall in London's Portobello Road!

"She hid her astonishment however, and quickly planned how she might use this plum that had dropped in her lap to her own advantage. She persuaded them to leave the amulet with her, promising to clean it carefully and to try to find some secret buyer for it.

"Ladies and gentlemen, Phaedra did not clean the amulet, she merely substituted the newer amulet, claiming that her efforts had removed some of the centuries-old grime that had become imbedded in the piece. Remember, these are not educated men; they are herders and an inn keeper, owner of the Pensione Anastasia in Olympia, far removed from Athens. They fell for her ruse completely. After all, she was a relative of the family.

"She gave them the name of a dealer in London whom they might contact to sell the piece. When they asked her if she could act as agent for them, she told them she would be unable to help. Her jewelry business would keep her close to home in Corinth for the foreseeable future. So they left, not suspecting her of any wrong-doing.

"Meanwhile, the member of the group who owns Pensione Anastasia in Olympia, had an idea. His pensione at the time was expecting a group of students from London touring Greek temple sites with their professor, Maria Crawford. The innkeeper thought he could get the amulet to London in one of the students' cases. His son, a travel agent working on Charlotte Street in London, could intercept it and take it to the dealer in stolen art. The group members were desperate for money to further their political aims of course, and the amulet seemed like an unexpected gift from the gods.

"But the innkeeper underestimated Miss Emma Darling, a member of the university group. She refused pointblank to carry a package of *baklava* in which they secretly planned to hide the amulet. So they decided to hide the amulet in her case anyway, mark the case in a distinctive way, so it could be plucked off the carousel quickly by the travel agent in London once it arrived at Heathrow.

"By mistake, the wrong case was marked. Somehow the amulet ended up in Miss Darling's case, which was unmarked. The marked case, belonging to another student, Miss Jane Hale, was stolen instead. But it contained no amulet. Emma Darling's flat was then searched, she was sent threatening notes, but in the end she found the amulet herself and turned it over immediately to Scotland Yard." Here Charlie pauses for more tea.

"Shortly after that, Miss Darling helped us tremendously by locating the travel agent who had gone into hiding in London, and by also helping expose one of the ringleaders from Greece, who had flown to London to try to get possession of the amulet.

"As you probably have read in the newspapers, he has been deported. And the travel agent has a court appearance scheduled in several weeks. I personally hope that he will not face a prison term. I believe that this young man can be rehabilitated. There is strong evidence that he was an unwilling participant in the scheme, and was pressured by his family in the extreme.

"But I get ahead of myself. Back in Greece, George Soutakis is frantic when he discovers the amulet has been stolen. Because he had no heirs, he had decided the time had come to present the precious amulet to his country.

"He surprises Miss Crawford and her group of students while they are touring the temple of Bassae, accusing them of stealing it. But she is able to calm him, reassuring him of their innocence. Moreover she offers to try to help him recover the amulet. She contacts the Athens police, and they promise to talk with him and help in the search.

"Next George Soutakis appears at a doctor's dispensary in Delphi where Dr. McGregor, traveling with Miss Crawford's group, has gone to seek treatment for one of the university students who suffered a broken bone in her foot while clambering over the ruins at Delphi. He overhears the shepherd tell the doctor someone pushed rocks off a ledge over his head, trying to kill him as he walked below, but he sustained only minor injuries which the Greek doctor treated, and subsequently sent him on his way.

"The following day when the students are visiting Constitution Square in Athens prior to their departure for London, a car careening out of control strikes a pedestrian in the crosswalk then speeds away.

"The victim is George Soutakis, but a man with a much changed appearance: clean-shaven, neatly cut hair, wearing a new shirt and trousers and carrying a briefcase. We believe he was advised by the police to adopt such a disguise because they feared something like this might happen.

"Dr. McGregor, who happened to be sitting at one of the outdoor cafes surrounding the square, rushes to aid him and reaches him just before he dies, hears him whisper the words 'going to Heathrow' as he expires, a tragic end to a man who was a real patriot. We believe George Soutakis learned the amulet was bound for Heathrow sometime shortly before he died.

"Phaedra Patakis has now confessed to driving the car in Constitution Square that fateful day. The Athens police tell us the vehicle is registered in her name. Apparently Soutakis obtained information linking her to the amulet. Perhaps he suspected it was in her possession, and threatened her, frightening her badly. She decided to get rid of him and followed his movements to Constitution Square. She will be facing murder charges for his death, as she has confessed to driving the car which killed George Soutakis.

"Moving back in time, before her arrest, we find she plans to take the original amulet to London and sell it. Remember, the Greek-Cypriot group still has no inkling that she has double-crossed them by switching the amulets.

"She quietly schedules her trip to London, cleverly maneuvering to get in the good graces of the travel agent Michael Leonidas when she arrives, hoping to obtain information of the Greek-Cypriot group back in Greece from him. Above all, she not want to arouse suspicions that she has tricked them.

"But Michael Leonidas loses no time in letting her know that he has no wish to discuss the Greek Cypriot cause, or any of his relatives who support it. He has cut his ties with the political group once and for all and is determined to stay on the right side of the law. He wants no part of her scheming, but as a dutiful son, he remains on friendly terms with his cousin.

"Phaedra set up a meeting with Roberto Gubbio yesterday afternoon at the Man in the Moon pub on Portobello Road, a few feet away from her jewelry stall. An alert Emma Darling and her friend Jane Hale, whose suitcase was mistakenly stolen at Heathrow at the beginning of our story, discover her stall. They learn the woman has gone into the pub with a man described as a foreigner by the adjoining stall owner.

"They hurry to the pub and overhear enough of the conversation between Phaedra and Gubbio to realize that the sale of an amulet is taking place. Moreover they glimpse the amulet from their adjoining booth. They quickly alert Scotland Yard." Charlie smiles.

"But they fear the conspirators will get away before help arrives. They see a case filled with notes, seven hundred and fifty thousand pounds actually, and they see the amulet. But what to do? Miss Darling and Miss Hale, secreted in the booth behind, realize they will be no match for the pair." Here Charlie pauses, taking note of the tension and suspense at the table.

"Now ladies and gentlemen," he says, "what do you suppose extremity drives these young women to do? I will tell you. They saturate the unsuspecting criminals with beer, good British beer, raining down on their heads from upturned pitchers. In the ensuing pandemonium, Scotland Yard arrives, the conspirators are led away, the satchel of money and the amulet are saved.

"Both amulets, the original and the later copy, will be returning to Greece shortly, to enter the National Museum in Athens as George Soutakis wished." Charlie leans back, his account complete. Long and sustained applause breaks out. A flurry of questions pepper the air.

How did Phaedra come to the attention of the Bassae Shepherd? Why didn't the Greek-Cypriots suspect her of switching the amulets? Was there not a vast difference in appearance of the two works of art? How can Scotland Yard be sure about the travel agent Mike Leonidas? He did not volunteer information about Phaedra to them, did he? Charlie smiles and holds up his hands.

"First question: We actually do not yet know what put George Soutakis on to Phaedra. Perhaps he followed the political group when they took the amulet to her to be evaluated. Whatever it was, it was enough to make him highly suspicious. As for the group, they thought of Phaedra first because she was a relative. She was related to the innkeeper's wife, remember? More importantly, she was available. Remember, these are hill people. They have no connections with the art world whatsoever.

"Why didn't they suspect her of switching amulets? There was no knowledge of a second amulet, remember. No one, certainly no one in the remote mountains of rural Greece, knew copies had been made. Also, the difference in the two pieces is not so obvious as you might think, especially when they are viewed separately. To the thieves, there was only one amulet and a jeweler they knew had cleaned it. Only Phaedra knew the truth.

"As for Michael Leonidas, you are right, he did not come to the police with information about his cousin because she did not reveal to him the amulet was in her possession! She had to keep that from him at all costs. The conspirators would be after her if they knew. What she wanted from Michael was information. She gave out none in return, and she was to him a relative who must, for courtesy's sake, be shown around London, nothing more."

As the questions ebb and flow around her Emma thinks to herself: so it is finally over. The real amulet by Phidias will go back to Greece. Relief is overwhelming. She feels a torpor, an exhaustion induced by a nagging tension which has gripped her ever since returning from Greece. Dimly she is aware of Professor Martin and Sir Lionel discussing reasons why the amulet is most likely genuine. And Emma is aware of Sam, sitting near her, his eyes filling with pride as he looks at her.

In spite of her earlier resolve, the thought brazenly presents itself: I love him! Quickly she pushes it away, like a troublesome gnat on a humid summer afternoon in Virginia, but the thought persists. I love Sam. And no matter how determined her will, the little words repeat themselves over and over like some chant from a childhood game.

Her mind wanders. She sees herself returning to America to take up a curatorial post in some unknown city. It has always been her long-cherished dream, but she finds now it means as little to her as a favorite melody played too often which suddenly becomes trite, ordinary, meaningless.

Oh, my heart. What tricks the heart can play. And what of dreams, plans, goals for success she has tried to keep uppermost in her mind? They now seem insignificant incidentals to be brushed aside.

She becomes aware of Jane's hand on her arm. "Emma, everyone's leaving," she whispers.

Emma quickly speeds her thoughts to the present and joins the little group moving toward the door. Soon only she and Jane are left with Charlie and Sam. Emma knows Sam's time is limited; he is on duty at Guy's tonight.

"I thought we might offer you a quick birthday drink at the bar, Charlie," Sam says. "Guiness, perhaps?" He looks innocently at Jane and Emma.

"Sam, you are a beast! Emma and I will carry the horrid taint to our graves! But a drink in honor of Charlie's birthday? Yes, surely," Jane adds.

"That would be topping," Charlie answers. "I was forced to cancel my birthday lunch with the Mater and Pater because of this little tea party. To tell the truth, I've barely had time to catch a few winks since I left you two on Portobello Road. I've been beavering away into the wee hours on this business."

Seated at a small table in comfortably overstuffed chairs, they watch as Jane shyly presents Charlie with the seal, still neatly wrapped in Mr. Spratt's brown paper. Emma can see Charlie is touched.

"It's handsome, Jane. Where on earth did you find it?" he exclaims. "Jolly nice, Jane." He kisses her lightly on the cheek.

"Actually at Mr. Daniel C. Spratt's stall on PB Road. His stall happened to be next to Phaedra's, and he's the one who directed us to the pub. He said she'd gone there with a 'furriner'," Jane adds. "Finding the seal brought us luck."

"Oh, Emma, You are *my* 'furriner'. What am I going to do with my beer-guzzling American?" Sam asks, turning toward Emma in a proprietary way, as Jane and Charlie exchange glances.

"I don't know, Sam," Charlie speaks up. "That's entirely up to you, and to Emma of course. But I do know this, she can carve out a niche for herself at the Yard if she ever feels she wants to go in that direction." Charlie's voice holds respect.

As they sit silently for a minute. Emma, alone with her dreams, thinks: are the four of us to end up like one of Shakespeare's plays, recalling various pairs of the dramatist's happy lovers, Hermia and Lysander? Petruchio and Katherine? Beatrice and Benedick? The prospect is pleasing to her as she sits, holding Sam's hand.

TEN

Coffee near the British Museum

After a series of postponements, the students hold their reunion at the Gower Street Cafe, fondly called The Caff. London newspapers have been running frequent features on the Apollo Amulets; the friends have many questions for Emma and Jane. Emma wishes Miss Crawford could be present to help answer all their questions. But she knows the lecturer rarely fraternizes with her students.

"Just think," cries Primrose Wise, looking soulful in thick-lens glasses, "They're going back to Greece, both of them. The amulets will ever be a part of our memories of Bassae." The amulets are indeed on their way to the National Museum in Athens.

Brian Gibbs proudly tells the group he has turned over several hundred photos of the trip to Miss Crawford who will narrow the field to seventy or so for their book collaboration on Greek temple sites. Gee's foot is still cocooned in the cast. Her broken bone is healing nicely and she now maneuvers effortlessly on the crutches.

Jocelyn and Rosamund have applied to study art history for a term at the Sorbonne in Paris in the autumn. Emma tells them she plans sending off letters and resumes to museums in the United States, hoping to garner job interviews. But she does not reveal that her enthusiasm for going back to America has dimmed somewhat, now that she and Sam are closer. And Jane announces that she has applied to Birkbeck College in London, to study art history beginning in the fall.

"But that's wonderful, Jane," says Emma in surprise. "You'll be right here in London. Isn't that where you want to be?" Jane, blushing, nods. Charlie, Emma thinks. Jane and Charlie, but she is not ready to say anything, yet.

The group feels carefree, now that final papers are safe in the hands of Miss Crawford. Only the final examination, a four-hour written paper on an undisclosed subject, looms ahead of them in August. Speculation descends to the ridiculous as they try to guess what the set subject will be when they sit down in the examination room to take up their pens and begin.

"How to Survive a Diet of Barbecued Goat in Greece," Brian Gibbs suggests with sly glances in Jane's direction. "First Aid for Broken Bones at Temple Sites," and "A Handbook for Mastering Greek Pensione Plumbing" are some of the other suggested titles. The joking does not obscure the fact that they all know the final exam will be a monster in its complexity with nothing frivolous in its makeup.

Vast mountains of chips are consumed. The little group discovers what they shared in Greece has bound them closer together. How I wish Sam could be here, Emma thinks. Wishing each other good luck on the examination, the friends scatter, Emma and Jane leisurely walking past the BM and on to Oxford Circus where they pause to look in Liberties window.

Emma's eyes fall on a pewter art nouveau teapot and she asks Jane to go in with her to look at it. "It would be perfect for the Belfrages as a homecoming present," she says. "They have been wonderful hosts to me, and they return from France in a few days."

The teapot costs sixty pounds. Seeing Emma's face fall, the perceptive clerk guides her to a display of earthenware teapots, pointing out one in a similar shape, designed by a young British potter. The price is twenty-two pounds.

"Not nearly so dear," the shop assistant smiles at her, "and really, earthenware brews a better pot of tea."

Emma makes the purchase, hugging it tightly as she and Jane descend into the Underground to catch the Piccadilly line for Knightsbridge.

Riding in the tube, Jane confides that she is taking a small flat on Russell Square for the autumn onward. Would Emma consider sharing with her? Her father has been extremely generous.

"The rent will not be much," she promises.

Emma cannot believe Jane's news. What bliss, to live with Jane in her very own flat in London! But she will have to find some sort of a job in order to extend her stay. She won't ask her parents to support her. She must earn her way. After all, her year of study is almost over. But she would love to stay on until January, when Sam leaves for Aberdeen.

"It sounds heavenly, Jane," she says. "Let me think it over."

They come up from the tube at Knightsbridge and go their separate ways. Emma strolls in a leisurely way toward Chesham Place, turning into the key garden across from the Carleton Tower hotel. Inside the gardens she can see tennis games in progress on the two courts, overhung by large plane trees. At one end of the garden, a play area has been built, where mothers bring small children to romp and enjoy a few moments to chat with friends.

"Stand clear, Fiona, while I give Nigel a swing." A young mother's soft voice floats in the air.

"Mummy! My sand castle crumbled away!" Emma listens to the high pitched little voices of the children and lets herself dream of a blond-haired boy and his sister, tiny replicas of Sam, playing in a London park while she keeps watch.

Yes, it has a definite appeal, Emma muses, smiling to herself as she continues to stroll aimlessly in the key garden, admiring pink hydrangeas blooming along the iron railings. Life could certainly be very pleasant, living in London with Sam.

She thinks of Crozet and the layered hills of the Blue Ridge, her home, and a lump rises in her throat. How she loves Virginia! There the cicadas will already be singing their sad song of goodbye, for autumn and cooler nights are swiftly coming, along with mornings heavy with mist. When autumn truly arrives with colder nights, then the Blue Ridge trees will exchange green dresses for brilliant reds, oranges and yellows before finally casting their finery to the ground.

Does everyone have such unsettling thoughts when they grow up, facing important decisions about what to do with one's life? She wonders if the time has finally arrived to leave her home in America? She sighs, shifts the parcel holding the teapot, lets herself out of the gate, being sure it clicks shut.

As she enters the flat on Chesham Place, the telephone is ringing.

"Emma, Charlie here." Undisguised excitement in his voice.

"Why Charlie, I thought Jane said you had an unexpected trip to Athens."

"Yes, I'm still here," he answers. "I'll be flying back to London later tonight. Emma, would you be free to come to Greece in late August for the presentation ceremonies of the two amulets? The officials here want you, Jane, Miss Crawford and Sam. They will pick up the tab, of course. And this isn't your official invitation, by the way. We're just getting a count of who can make it."

Emma's head is spinning as she quickly thinks of the timing. "I could do, Charlie. Our exam is the fifteenth of August. Any time after that would be fine." Although she says nothing, she is worrying. Will Sam be able to get away?

"Splendid, Emma. I'll give the others a tinkle. Goodbye for now."

Emma holds the telephone in her hands. What a fantastic piece of luck. And Sam invited too! It will be a fitting finale to the episode of the Apollo Amulets. Her thoughts turn to the final examination. A whole year of study is riding on that exam. She can't afford to flub it. She needs to buckle down on her revision. After the exam, she can dream about Athens.

Jane and Emma decide to meet each morning at the key garden on Sloane Street to do their revision. They are lucky the Belfrages own a key. England is enjoying one of the warmest and driest summers on record. People are flocking daily to the parks soaking up the sun. Pale bodies lounge, clad in the skimpiest of tops and shorts. Canvas chairs are available to rent by the day at all London parks. With such a few really sunny days, it's hardly feasible to own one, plus the bother of carrying it back and forth to one's flat.

Some Londoners with tender northern skins, redheads especially, go about with bad cases of sunburn. Emma and Jane turn pleasing tones of brown as they study in the gardens, Jane wearing a big straw sun hat to protect her sensitive skin which develops freckles easily.

"Tell me about the Kouros figures," Emma says, and Jane responds with characteristics, dates and styles. Locations of the most famous ones are imprinted firmly in their minds.

"Tell me about the lost chryselephantine statue of Zeus by Phidias," Jane asks Emma, and on it goes.

They review components of all the most important temples of ancient Greece. Around them, subdued by the barrier of trees and shrubs, the traffic of central London hums. Their ears grow accustomed to the frequent screeching of taxi brakes, the rumbling of the giant double-decker buses. The garden's verdant band of insulation muffles the sound and makes it seem far away. They are aware of the pleasant thwack of tennis balls from nearby courts and the soft voices of children in the playground area.

On one occasion when they linger until lunchtime in the garden, they are joined by a multigenerational Indian family gathering for a family picnic. Colorful bedspreads are flung on the ground. The women, brilliant as parrots and toucans in saris of red, green and yellow, unpack tiffins, lunch baskets. The men lounge on the ground, some with long hair carefully tucked under silk turbans draped in complicated folds. The beautiful, dark-eyed children circle around them, playing endless games of tag.

Emma has not seen Sam in a week, but it seems more like a month to her. He is going through an especially busy time at Guy's and his registrar is withholding permission for him to make the trip to Athens until he secures a replacement.

Sam is consumed by frustration. In addition to being badly overworked, he has heard nothing yet from the paper he submitted earlier. Privately he agrees with Emma who thinks it unfair for him to be denied the trip to Athens. After all, he has been chosen to represent Britain. And if he does win the competition for Aberdeen, he needs to begin making plans for his move to Scotland in January. Summer is ebbing away.

Emma and Jane have a rule that they won't indulge in personal talk until they finish revising for the day. Sometimes, it is a difficult rule to keep, especially when they long to talk over the proposed trip to Athens. What to wear? Where will they be staying? Whom will they meet?

"Charlie says they are putting us up at one of the big hotels at Constitution Square," Jane reveals. "We'll only be there two nights. The presentation ceremony will be the first morning after we arrive. There's a special luncheon I believe, then we have a free evening and fly out the next day."

"It sounds marvelous," Emma says. "We are so lucky, we should pinch ourselves."

"Just think, it's because of Charlie that we're making the trip. I feel sure he must have suggested it to them, the Greeks I mean." Jane's voice fills with pride as she speaks. Emma smiles. He is clearly the apple of her eye. Her own thoughts turn to Sam.

"It's so unfair. I am beginning to think that Sam's horrid registrar doesn't want him to go." Emma's eyes blaze. Jane looks at her quickly, surprised at her depth of feeling.

"Why Emma, you really care about him, don't you?"

"So much, Jane. So very much," Emma whispers, dabbing at her eyes with a tissue.

"Silly, but I never realized," Jane falters. "You are always so cool when he's around. I had no idea. I knew you liked him, but . . ."

"That's what's so maddening," Emma replies. "I care too much to act cool anymore. I'm loosing my self-possession. And Sam does not have a clue how I feel." She twists her hands in her lap, consumed by tension.

"Why don't you tell him just what you've told me?" Jane asks "I'm sure he feels the same way."

"I can't," Emma replies helplessly. "Here I am, a grown woman, and I cannot announce to him how much he means to me. We've talked about nothing but my going back to America, carving out a niche in the museum world. In a way, part of me still wants to do that. But another part keeps thinking of Sam and how dreadful it's going to be when we have to say goodbye. I'm so muddled, Jane. And I never ever thought of myself as indecisive. In fact, I've often let myself despise uncertainty in other people."

"You're not indecisive," Jane speaks up loyally. "Not in a million years. Things will come right between you and Sam, I know they will. If you'd noticed how he looked at you at Charlie's tea party at Browns Hotel, you'd understand how he feels. Sam is waiting for the proper time to speak, but I have no doubt it will be soon."

They gather up their papers, finished for the day. Somewhat comforted, Emma realizes having a friend like Jane is one of the nicest things that has happened to her since arriving in England.

~

Emma feels like a hit and run victim as she staggers out of the examination room, hurries along the corridor then down the steps of London University's Examination Building, gratefully breathing in the polluted air of Gower Street in great gulps. The ordeal is over!

"This is unreal," she mumbles, leaning on the railing alongside the wide steps. She feels numb, drained after the four hours at that desk, in that room, desperately writing, desperately thinking. She clasps and unclasps her right hand, dimly aware of the numbness and pain.

"You look flattened," Sam's voice at her elbow dissolves her self-absorption. He gives her a quick hug and guides her along the walk.

"You hurried right past me, Emma. I could have been a lamp post. A bit hard on a chap who's been waiting for over half an hour, wouldn't you say?"

She shakes her head murmuring, "So sorry, Sam. I'm comatose after four hours. But thanks so much for being here to collect the pieces."

"What was the question?" he asked. "Jane came out a few seconds before you, but I didn't have the heart to ask. She looked knackered and hurried off to lick her wounds in private."

"We had to rank six Greek Temples in the order of their importance, giving reasons to support the claim. Really a tough one. And Jane and I had worked so hard on sculpture in our revision. Now I wish we'd covered the architectural side more." She looks wistfully at him.

"Don't go looking back. It's over and done and I'm sure you did well. Forget it, let's get some coffee."

Sam guides her as they turn into Museum Street. He makes for a little cafe near the British Museum, quickly finds two seats at a tiny table and returns with steaming mugs of coffee. Emma sips hers silently. After finishing, she sits back, equanimity restored. She looks at Sam and smiles.

"What about you, Sam. Any news of a replacement for you at Guy's?"

"Yes," he replies. "My motives in meeting you after your ordeal weren't entirely selfless. I have good news. The Registrar has found someone to take my place. I can go to Athens." Impulsively Emma places her hand over his on the little marble-top table.

"I am glad," she says simply, looking into his eyes.

His eyes hold hers. "There's something else, Emma. I just received word this morning. I've been offered the place at Aberdeen at the teaching hospital, beginning in January."

So soon. It means their time together will now begin draining away. No matter how much longer she stays in London, Sam will be leaving in January. Quickly Emma hides her feelings and smiles her brightest smile.

"Sam, that's wonderful. Congratulations." But even as the words come out of her mouth, her heart sinks.

Emma feels a knot tighten in her stomach. Why does she sit there pretending it is wonderful when it means he will be leaving? Going to a different world, far away from her. Slowly hopes trickle away, like water vanishing down a drain. She wills herself to smile at the spot above Sam's eyes, carefully avoiding looking into them. She must hide her sadness, even if it kills her.

"So you'll be leaving soon after we get back from Christmas holidays," she says.

"Wait, wait. I haven't accepted yet." He senses her struggle for composure. "I need time to consider. I suppose, if I really wanted, I could stay on at Guy's. The pay isn't as good, but London is London." He speaks slowly, studying her face as though looking for a clue to her inner feelings. "After all, you are here, Emma, and try as I might, I have trouble imagining you in Aberdeen."

"Why is that, Sam?" Emma asks, genuinely hurt. "You seem uncertain about my ability to be happy anywhere but London, or New York or Washington. You are wrong."

"But Aberdeen is so provincial, not a city like Edinburgh, which has wonderful art and theater. Then too, there's the cold. All of Scotland is very cold in winter. The winters are dark, wet and never-ending. I have trouble picturing you north of Oxford, Emma."

"Not fair, Sam. My state of Virginia has cold winters. It's not sub tropical, like Florida." Emma feels herself dangerously near tears. She bites her lip. "This wrangling is pointless." He nods absent-mindedly.

"The beauty of taking the post in Aberdeen is not only the experience I would gain. It would also mean a leg up if I wanted to come back to London after I've finished. Then too, the stipend is very good. It would allow me to put aside a sizable chunk for my younger brothers, if they decide to get busy with their A levels." Emma's heart plummets.

"Then you must go." Emma says it quickly. "Of course you must go. You owe it to yourself, and to them." She carefully ignores the knot in her stomach. She will not let Sam see how her world has suddenly catapulted topsy-turvy.

"And you, Emma Darling, what do I owe to you?" Sam whispers softly. The way he says it, her surname sounds like an endearment, and suddenly as though a tap has been turned on, two large tears well in her eyes and roll slowly down her cheeks. Ashamed at her weakness, she gropes frantically in her shoulder bag for a tissue.

"No, you mustn't think of me. Remember, I'll be going soon too," she says quickly. Sam slides his chair very close to hers in the deserted cafe, tilts her chin and looks into her eyes.

"Going where, Emma Darling?" he asks, speaking her name again in that wonderful way, looking into her eyes. "Where are you going?"

"I'm not sure" she falters, grasping at something solid and matter of fact. "You know I've already been working on letters and my resume, for a job in America." Her voice trails off and she falls silent. She is not sure how to frame what she wishes to say to him at this moment. But she knows, she cannot be the first one to speak of her love for him. It is a horrid burden, but that is what she is, the way she is made.

"Listen," Sam says, whispering, while behind them, the owner of the cafe busily begins the routine of closing. They are the only customers remaining. "You have become a part of my life, Emma, and I want to keep you there. Maybe we don't know when or where yet, but one day I want to marry you. Take you home to meet my family near Edinburgh, introduce you to my Registrar, who isn't such a bad chap, by the way. I want to marry you. I love you."

There, he has said it, words she has been longing to hear. The words that mean he really does care for her.

"I want you to be Dr. McGregor's wife, the mother of little McGregors. Do you understand?" Sam leans back, looks at her.

Understand? Of course she does. The words are like some sublime Bach chorus she wills herself to hear over and over again. Now she knows she will have the strength to endure the separation or whatever it takes to rearrange their lives so that they will be together sometime, somewhere. The place is no longer important.

"I understand, Sam," Emma says simply. "I love you too."

They sit quietly, hand in hand until a deferential, unassuming owner, now minus his white apron, approaches the little table.

"Sir, Miss," he begins, "This cafe does mainly lunchtime trade. I live in Pinner and must catch the train to get home in time to make the *taramousalata* and *baklava* fresh for tomorrow. Can you come back another time? We close at five."

Sam, glancing at his watch and noting that it is already five fifteen, jumps up and apologizes, saying they are very sorry and hadn't realized it was closing time. Then, looking at the name of the cafe on the awning, George's Place, he adds, "George, you've no idea how happy being in your cafe has made us today! We will be back."

"Oh yes, we will," Emma adds in voice like the pealing of distant bells as together they float out of the cafe and down Museum Street. George, short, stocky and greying, married for many years, gazes fondly after them, remembering being young in another place, another time. He locks the door and cranks up the awning before scurrying away to the tube station.

Sam and Emma walk, realizing that each step brings the moment of parting closer. They continue the length of Oxford Street, entering Hyde Park at Speakers Corner, cutting across the park toward Knightsbridge. Sam veers with Emma slightly off the path where, behind a stunning bed of towering blue delphinium, he kisses her soundly.

"So, Emma Darling," he says playfully as they continue, "Do you think you can consent to marry me? At some future date, that is?"

"Yes, Sam." The words tumble out. She experiences a little leap of joy. because she has given the gift of her deepest feelings to him.

They decide to say nothing to anyone, but to keep their news a secret until plans are more certain. They part at the Knightsbridge tube station, Sam taking the underground to Guy's Hospital, Emma walking toward Chesham Place. When she finally reaches the flat, she gives Frances Belfrage a glowing account of the examination paper.

Later that evening when Frances relates this to her husband as they sit in the yellow kitchen over coffee, she muses, "I don't think I've ever seen Emma so animated. She really must have done well on that exam."

~

On the day of the appearance of Michael Leonidas in magistrate court in Soho, Charlie alerts Jane and Emma, thinking they might wish to appear to give him support. The session is already underway when they arrive and slip quietly into seats behind Alexis Sobranos. Mike's case will come up next on the docket she whispers to Emma. Peter Ackroyd, solicitor, looks smoothly confident in a Savile Row suit with matching shirt and tie from Jermyn Street, signature street for gentlemen's haberdashery in London.

Mike, wearing a brown suit of a more conventional cut, sits at the table with his solicitor. He looks worried and nervous. He glances toward Alexis and sees Jane and Emma behind, beaming smiles of encouragement.

Charlie is called to testify. Clearly and carefully, he tells the court how Mike has cooperated fully with police, fulfilling conditions outlined by Scotland Yard. Next Charlie builds on Mike's unblemished character. Smoothly he segues into Mike's faithfully sending money home to his family all the years he has been in London. And he points out Mike has no blemish on his record whatsoever during his residence in Britain.

Next Charlie tells the court something Emma has not known. Mike came to Charlie one afternoon after they had met earlier on Charlotte Street for a quick bite of lunch. At the later meeting, Mike told Charlie about his Greek cousin, Phaedra Patakis, who had arrived in London for some unknown purpose, and although he did not know what it was, he was almost certain it was unlawful. This information was extremely valuable. It pointed suspicion toward the woman later apprehended with the original amulet in her possession. The woman has now confessed and will face charges of theft and murder in Greece.

Charlie goes on to inform the court of the incident at Heathrow, followed by Mike's posing as a window cleaner and entering the flat in Belgravia. Charlie is careful to note that in each instance, nothing whatsoever was taken by Michael Leonidas. The incidents are seen by Charlie as results of unreasonable threats and demands from his uncle Scopas and his family in Greece. The facts speak for themselves: two, not one, amulets have been recovered and returned to Greece. Moreover, a murderer has been caught with help from the defendant. Charlie believes this should weigh heavily in Mike's favor.

Peter Ackroyd, solicitor for the accused, speaks. Surely the Crown cannot in any way be threatened by Michael Leonidas. He has exhibited exemplary behavior and deserves to be set free of all restrictions. He moves for a dismissal. The venerable, bewigged old magistrate, nodding behind thick lenses of his spectacles, suddenly perks up. Not wanting to be late for a luncheon engagement in Mayfair, he quickly pronounces a dismissal.

It is over. Alexis and Mike meet in the corridor outside the courtroom and embrace. Alexis turns quickly to Jane and Emma and together she and Mike thank them for their support.

"She'll keep her eye on him," Charlie drawls as the couple walks away in the warm sunlight, arm in arm.

"Mike said when I asked him about his family that his father may go to prison for his part in the conspiracy," Emma reveals as they watch them leave. "I certainly hope not, now that Phaedra has confessed to running down the Bassae Shepherd. What will happen to Pensione Anastasia if he receives a prison sentence?"

"I haven't heard any later news about that." Charlie says. "Hopefully we can find out something when we get to Athens."

"The sister Lydia is staying in Athens, Charlie, with Alexis Sobranos' family. Did you know?" Jane asks. Charlie raises his eyebrows.

"What did I tell you?" he grins at the girls. "A good woman is worth her weight in gold. Now let's go have a Chinese, what do you say? I'm a bit peckish and Soho has great Chinese restaurants on every corner."

ELEVEN

Summer Finale in Athens

Returning to the marble encased, dark and oppressive airport at Athens, Emma feels an undefined sense of foreboding. She dislikes the shadowy look of all that grey marble, the unfriendly customs officials, the surly baggage men. Is this the Greece she loves so much?

Their flight was late leaving Heathrow and when it finally took off, she and Jane fell asleep at once, to the murmured conversation of Sam, Charlie and Miss Crawford sitting in the row behind them. Emma fights for consciousness like a drowning swimmer when the flight attendant gently taps her shoulder.

"We're landing in a few minutes, Miss."

Speeding toward their hotel in a taxi with Jane and Sam, Emma only wishes to sink back into the oblivion of sleep. Charlie and Miss Crawford follow in a taxi behind them and together they arrive at the imposing facade of the Athena Palace on Constitution Square. Check-in is swift, and after brief goodnights, they hurry to their rooms, arranging to meet downstairs at nine the following morning.

Sleepily Emma unpacks, hangs up her dresses, and readies herself for bed. "Take the bed nearest the window, Emma," says Jane, collapsing on the bed near the door. Gratefully Emma sinks down, hardly noticing the attractive blue bed coverings and curtains, she is so weary.

Emma awakes early as bright sunlight streams through the sheer curtains. Refreshed by sound sleep, she has recovered her usual sense of well-being. This will be the last great adventure of summer, she realizes, watching dancing patterns made by the sunlight reflected on the room's ceiling. Quietly she tiptoes to the bureau where her shoulder bag rests. She takes out the long white envelope which has been at the back of her mind ever since it arrived in yesterday's post. She reads,

Dear Miss Darling:

We read with interest your letter of application and your qualifications as set forth in your resume. It seems as if you might be the person we are seeking for the post of assistant curator opening in January, 1976. With this in mind we would like to interview you as soon as possible. Is there a date when you would be available? We would also appreciate your sending the name and address of your professor at London University so we can write for additional information. If you plan a trip to the States in the autumn, perhaps we could schedule the interview at that time.

I look forward to your reply.

Yours sincerely,
David Sandborn, Chief Curator,
Corcoran Gallery of Art, Washington DC

Emma sighs. Well here it is, the chance at a dream job I've been working toward for the last five years. But strangely the prospect does not shine with the luster she had anticipated. Could it be she has somewhat outgrown, gone beyond, this drive to succeed which has played such an important role in all her efforts up to this time? Life has now become a configuration in which Sam plays a leading role. She taps the letter on her knee. She will tell no one about it yet, except of course Miss Crawford. She will need to meet with her soon, to ask her to send a letter of recommendation.

Coffee and croissants arrive and she and Jane breakfast hurriedly in their room, rushing downstairs at nine o'clock. The ceremony of the unveiling of the amulets is set for ten o'clock at the National Museum. Because of the oppressively high temperatures of Greece in August, Emma and Jane, advised by Alexis, wear cool, loose fitting cottons.

When they meet downstairs in the lobby, they encounter Miss Crawford, resplendent in grey linen. Charlie wears a jaunty suit made of a pin striped seersucker while Sam looks cool and collected in a summer weight suit of pale beige.

Their two taxis at the foot of the steps of the great museum are met by the director, Plato Christophorus, slender, dark-haired, with friendly brown eyes and a slightly rumpled look to his suit. He greets them warmly, particularly Maria Crawford, whom he has met several times before.

"Welcome to the Museum, and to Greece. We will proceed at once to the small gemstone gallery where the ceremony will take place as soon as the Minister of Culture arrives. His name, by the way, is Aristotle Pandapolous. So," he smiles broadly, "You are meeting at one time a Plato and an Aristotle. You must be in Greece, eh!"

Plato ushers them inside. As they walk toward the gem gallery, Emma recalls her recent visit to the National Museum. Only a few weeks ago, but it seems deep in the past, for so much has happened. Christophorous leads the way, talking in an animated tone with Miss Crawford.

Again Emma admires the massive bronze sculpture of a man from the Artemisium Wreck, the sculpture brought up from the sea. Emma, looking at the sightless eyes feels moved as before. She spies the bronze sculpture of the young jockey, an enduring symbol of the greatness of early Greek art. Seeing the sculptures is like seeing old friends.

They reach the gem galleries. In the center of the room stands a large glass cabinet over which a curtain had been draped. Tapping heels in the marble corridor behind them signal the arrival of the Minister of Culture and his entourage. A small contingent of people carrying notebooks follow in his wake. They wear cards labeled 'Press' on their lapels. The ceremony will be private with members of the public being admitted immediately following its conclusion.

After introductions are complete, Plato Christophorus begins to address the small group which includes a few of the higher ranking members of the museum's staff.

"It is with the greatest gratitude and pride that we gather here this morning to reveal the recently recovered Amulet of Apollo, a lost work by our Greek genius, Phidias, in the fifth century before Christ. This seems almost miraculous. Such events rarely happen today, rather we seem to preside over a diminution of precious antiquities rather than an increase." He pauses, smiling at the group.

"The presence of the Amulet of Apollo in these galleries will greatly enhance this museum's already rich assembly of treasures. Indeed every person of this country is enriched by its arrival on our shores." He pauses to let his words sink in.

"Now May I present to you our distinguished Minister of Culture, Mr. Aristotle Pandapolous."

The Minister of Culture is partly bald and portly with twinkling eyes set in a face of great character. He is a wonderful grandfather figure, Emma thinks as he walks to the center of the room, to stand beside the curtained case.

"Friends," he begins, "I have two duties to perform on this momentous and felicitous occasion. The first is to recognize and to honor four citizens of Great Britain and one citizen of the United States, all of whom have helped us in the recovery of the amulet and its return to Greece. Miss Edith Maria Crawford, Dr. Samuel Hamish McGregor, Mr. Charles Edward St. Cyr, Miss Jane Elizabeth Catherine Hale and Miss Emma Lorraine Darling: will you please come forward?"

And as the five stand before him he places over their heads silver medals, replicas of the amulet suitably engraved and threaded onto blue ribbons. When applause dies down, he continues.

"There is a sixth medal, to be awarded posthumously, to one of our own countrymen, the late George Soutakis, whose memory we honor in the naming of this amulet The George Soutakis Memorial Amulet. He gave his life not only for art, but for his country."

The curtains are eased away and the case containing the amulet is revealed. Enthusiastic applause breaks out. It is a moment to savor, thinks Emma, feeling her eyes well up. Flash bulbs go off as the ceremony ends and they leave the gallery, led by Plato Christophorus.

Reaching the entrance to the museum, they come upon a long line of visitors waiting in line to visit the gem galleries, hoping for an early look at both of the amulets displayed together in the same case. They break into spontaneous applause as the four British and one American file by. Many of them have followed the story of the amulets in the Athens papers.

Once outside, they are greeted by throngs of well-wishers, ordinary citizens of Athens, holding bouquets of garden flowers which they shyly bring forward and place in the arms of Jane, Emma and Miss Crawford. Single blossoms are tossed at them from the crowd. The applause continues, settling around Emma like a giant, comforting blanket.

"If I live to be ninety, I'll never, never forget this," Jane whispers to Emma as they stand receiving tributes from the crowd. Out of the corner of her eye, Emma glimpses a misty-eyed Sam. Even Charlie seems moved. Miss Crawford looks happily surprised by the spontaneous outpouring of sentiment.

And as Emma continues to gaze at the crowd, one face stands out near the front. She finds her eyes locked with those of Lydia Leonidas. Emma takes a few steps forward and Lydia joins her at the bottom of the steps.

"I saw your brother just yesterday, Lydia. He is well and I know he would want me to give you his love. The case against him has been dismissed." She hesitates. "Are you all right, Lydia?" Lydia is silent for a moment.

"Things are getting better now," she answers stiffly. "First I want you to know I did not know they planned to put anything in the *baklava*. They did not tell me that. My mother sent me to Athens when the Sobranos family invited me to come, so I missed the trouble with my uncle and my father. The Sobranos family has been so kind to me."

She gestures to a young girl beside her. "This is Flavia Sobranos."

"You must be Alexis's young sister," Emma says. "I saw Alexis yesterday too. She is well, and misses her family in Athens. I think you look very much like your sister, Flavia." The small girl smiles, pride shining in her eyes. Lydia bends toward Emma.

"I must let you know I am very sorry I asked you to carry the package," she blurts out. "I know it was wrong now, but at the time, my parents were all swept up in something they believed in, or thought they did. My father, my uncle, things are so mixed up." Sadness creeps upon Emma as she sees hurt and confusion in Lydia's eyes. Emma quickly takes her hand.

"Don't worry, Lydia. Things will be better soon, I hope. Let's just be friends, shall we? Maybe I'll see you when you come to London. And I'll never forget the wonderful memories of Pensione Anastasia. I hope I can come back someday."

As she moves on down the steps and through the crowd toward the waiting taxis, Emma is rewarded by seeing a smile break out on Lydia's face. She is too young to have experienced so much unhappiness. Emma waves to the small figure.

Taxis take the party to a large hotel off Syntagma Square for a festive luncheon with the Minister of Culture, lasting until mid-afternoon. On the taxi ride back to their hotel, Emma quietly approaches Miss Crawford about a short meeting with her before the evening's outing in the Plaka, the ancient district of Athens near the Acropolis.

"Why not drop by now, when we reach the hotel?" Miss Crawford replies. "That will leave the afternoon free if we meet at once."

"Now Emma, what's this all about?" says Miss Crawford as they settle in comfortable chairs in her hotel room. Emma takes out the letter and hands it to her.

"A very nice letter," she says, after scanning it quickly. "It sounds like a wonderful opportunity, wouldn't you say?"

"Yes," says Emma. "I wanted to ask you to write a letter of recommendation, if you are willing. And of course, I'd like permission to send Mr. Sandborn your name and address."

"Certainly. I'll write him at once and send a copy to you. I'll do it the moment we return to London."

Emma breathes a sigh of relief. So that is taken care of. If only she could be as certain herself of what sort of future she wishes to pursue. Of course, she may not even be offered the Corcoran position.

"So if you decide to stay on in London in the autumn, what will you do?" Miss Crawford asks. "By the way, your examination paper was outstanding. You'll be receiving a 'Distinction' when the grades come out. Er, both you and Miss Hale," she adds. "You know they're miserably slow about these things at the University." Emma feels her cheeks burn with pride. A Distinction!

"I am not sure what I shall be doing in the autumn," Emma admits. "I'd like to remain in London, however," she adds, thinking of Jane's offer, wondering what sort of job she might find for the immediate future.

"It would be nice to have a job. I haven't made any plans."

"You should make the most of your time in London. Let me see." Absent-mindedly Miss Crawford taps the letter on her cheek, deep in thought.

"Miss Hale is planning to study at Birkbeck. That's a program leading to a degree. They would not admit you only for a semester, I'm afraid, as places are so very scarce. That doesn't mean there isn't some other way to put your talents to good use.

"Wait a minute." Her face brightens. "Have you ever heard of the Celia Drummond School?"

Emma looks at her doubtfully. "Isn't that the school for girls that teaches secretarial courses and teaches modeling also? Isn't it a sort of finishing school?" Surely Miss Crawford isn't suggesting she enroll there.

"Yes, that's the one. A lot of families from the country send their daughters up to acquire a little polish, some useful job skills and also to become familiar with all the enrichments London has to offer. They also teach them how to dress, how to walk, and so on. Really, it's quite a useful program. Some of them become quite good secretaries, and the more glamorous ones have landed modeling jobs with some of the best fashion houses I believe. The point is, they have a very good program of art appreciation.

"The director William Clark is a friend of mine. He mentioned recently that he is looking for an art lecturer, someone who will take the girls on visits to all the major galleries, the V & A., the Tate, the National, the BM and so on. Then there are the smaller ones not so well known: Sir John Soane's Museum, Dulwich Picture Gallery, The Wallace Collection, Kenwood House. You would be showing them the paintings and sculpture of course. It would be a marvelous opportunity for you to become better acquainted with the many galleries in London. That would be valuable experience for you. He mentioned the pay, I can't recall now what it is, but I remember thinking 'That's jolly good,' not that lecturing on art history is a road to riches. Far from it!" She laughs heartily.

"So, I'll give him a tinkle when we return, shall I?" She wears the confident expression that all had been neatly settled, and I haven't said a word, Emma marvels silently.

"I would be so grateful, Miss Crawford," Emma replies, thinking how good it would be to earn money toward her expenses. Her parents would be pleasantly surprised and, best of all, she would extend her time in London by a few more months and would be near Sam. And of course, learning more about some of London's lesser known galleries and museums would be of great benefit.

Emma thanks her and eases out of the room. "We'll just be patient and see what happens," says Miss Crawford brightly as she reaches the door. But Emma knows Miss Crawford is firm in her mind that all is settled!

~

Dinner that evening is organized by Plato Christophorus. Planned as a very private and informal party, the only guests are the five visitors from London. The oldest part of Athens still inhabited, the Plaka, backs up to the Acropolis. Walking along its narrow, twisting streets, festively lit, with music spilling out into the warm night sky, Emma is reminded of European cities she has visited in the past with her parents. Restaurants and shops fill the Plaka. Their trip could not have had a more fitting end, she thinks as the group strolls from their hotel toward The Neptune, the restaurant chosen by Plato for the evening celebration.

Emma wears a pale green silk which, surprisingly, has emerged from her case almost wrinkle-free. It must have been the way Frances packed it, she thinks, remembering the sheets of tissue paper Frances Belfrage patiently pressed around the dress as she placed it in Emma's case. Extra trouble, but worth it, Emma decides.

Walking along with Sam toward the restaurant, she tells him of the letter she received from Washington, of her meeting with Miss Crawford and the possibility of a job with the Celia Drummond School.

"Which would mean you would be staying on in London this autumn. That's wonderful news, Emma. I was afraid you would be leaving before I took off for Aberdeen. I've heard of the Celia Drummond School. I think it has a good reputation in Scotland, for girls who are looking for something to occupy their time until marriage rolls around."

"Why Sam," Emma bristles, "what a typical male attitude."

A postcard picture springs to her mind of the girls on the recent trip to Greece, clustering like butterflies around Sam and Brian Gibbs, and how they had loved all the attention!

"The girls at Celia Drummond School are probably much more interested in finding a good job and being independent in a big city like London, rather than hunting for a husband." she answers pertly. Sam, although he utters not a word, seems unconvinced.

The entrance to the restaurant is nondescript but inside they find a dim, cool, attractively furnished interior. Snowy cloths on each table hold lighted candles. Huge terra cotta pots, filled with blazing masses of midsummer flowers, dot the flagstone floor leading to an outdoor terrace at the back of the restaurant. From their table on the terrace they look up to the spotlighted silhouette of buildings on the Acropolis. Here the great art and thinking of Western Civilization really began, Emma thinks.

Waiters bring tiny plates of shrimp kebabs grilled to perfection in all their succulent juices followed by the traditional Greek salad, then a main course of some delicious fish unfamiliar to Emma. A local fish, she is told.

After dessert of flaky pastry topped with yogurt and fresh fruit, the guests lean back, replete. Plato Christophorus clears his throat and begins to speak.

"I thought you might like to hear what I have been able to find out about George Soutakis," he begins.

"Indeed yes," replies Maria Crawford quickly. She has recounted to him their meeting with the shepherd at the ruins of the Temple of Bassae.

"He played a very important role in the recovery of the amulet," Plato looks at each of them as he speaks. "His humble beginnings disguised a great strength of character. His honesty and belief in himself will long serve as an inspiration to us. He died a hero's death, without a doubt.

"Apparently the antecedents of George Soutakis lived near the Temple of Apollo at Bassae for many centuries. They were herders, a few sheep, many goats. No vast amounts of land. But somewhere along the line the ages-old legend of a missing amulet of Apollo by Phidias became more than just a legend to them. It became a reality.

"We don't know of course how it happened. A Soutakis herder may have taken refuge from a storm in the cave where it was hidden, hollowed out a depression to build a fire, and found it then. That's only one of a thousand possibilities. You can invent dozens more.

"At any rate, from that time onward the secret, and the location of the hiding place, was passed on from father to eldest son, down to George. Now George had a problem. Not only was he the only son, he had never married, and the line would die out with him. He knew the time had come for him to turn over the treasure to his country.

"In the meager facts we have learned about George Soutakis one thing is clear: he devotedly loved Greece, his homeland. Far from being merely a herdsman, he read all the history books he could get his hands on, especially Greek history. He sailed off on a freighter as a young boy, circling the world several times. He learned to speak English as well as several other languages.

"Somewhere along the way, he fulfilled his lust for travel and returned to Bassae: to the hills he knew and loved. More and more the keeping of the amulet weighed on him. He felt responsible for its safety. In his mind it already belonged to the nation because he had long given up the hope that he might marry and produce an heir. And he was the last of his family line. He was preparing to turn it over when the thieves discovered the hiding place, possibly led there unwittingly by him, and stole the treasure.

"It is important that we understand the depth of his agitation when this happened. The amulet, in a strange way, had become an obsession. It is as though his entire reason for existing had been taken away, He became frantic. His one charge in life had been to guard the amulet, and he had failed.

"This was the mental condition of the man who accosted your group at the temple site of Bassae." Plato Christophorus looks at Maria Crawford.

"That explains his rather frightening performance at the site," she says. "He literally unraveled before our eyes."

"You are exactly right," Plato agrees, taking up the threads of the account. "He went to work determined more than ever to track down the perpetrators. As you know he appeared early one morning at the Pensione

Anastasia. He had them very worried indeed. Somehow he'd got wind of the Leonidas brothers and their possible involvement in the theft. What we do not know is what put him on to Phaedra Patakis. She apparently has no idea herself, or if she does, she's withholding it."

Plato shakes his head before going on. "But that woman is ruthless, ruthless, unlike the Leonidas brothers. For all their tough talk, violence was not a part of their plan. They wanted to avoid violence if at all possible. That is why the police were having so much trouble in linking them with the hit and run accident that was actually no accident.

"Yes, they would balk at murder, whereas Phaedra would go to any means to keep the amulet for herself. She told the authorities Soutakis came to her house and threatened her, perhaps he did. At any rate she says she was badly frightened and staged the accident to remove George Soutakis permanently. She almost escaped detection. Only one bystander gave a useful description of the car. Another came up with the first three letters of the license plates." Here Plato pauses for a sip of wine before continuing.

"Before the accident the police were interested in helping George Soutakis and had advised him to change his appearance, sent him to get a shave, a haircut and provided new clothes. When he was run down almost immediately afterward, they realized he was telling them the truth. But Phaedra quickly had the car repainted and this threw them off her trail for a long time. They were sure they had found the guilty parties when they came to the Leonidas brothers, but Scopas did not know how to drive a motor car at all, and Petrus possessed only a small rusty van, probably incapable of running as far as from Olympia to Athens.

"Only when she was sent back from London were the police able to discover Phaedra's role in the accident. They found traces of the original paint under the new red paint of her car. This made the description of the one witness match up. And so," he sighs dramatically, placing his hands on the table, "it is finally finished."

"What do you think will happen to Scopas and Petrus?" Jane asks. Plato shrugs.

"Everybody wonders, no? They'll probably face only token prison sentences. After all, the Greek-Cypriot cause is popular in Greece. The amulet is safe in the National Museum as Soutakis wished. The real villain in this piece is Phaedra."

"And Phaedra," asks Miss Crawford. "What will be her fate?"

"Greek justice is lenient, except when it comes to murder. Who knows? Still," he shakes his head slowly, "she is a woman."

"Poor Mike Leonidas, and his little sister Lydia." Emma says. "They were led into all of this by the father, and the uncle." Plato Christophorus looks blank.

Charlie quickly speaks up. "He is the innkeeper's son who is a travel agent in London. His sister worked as a waitress at the Pensione Anastasia. She's living in Athens now with friends."

"I suppose the pensione will close," Plato says, "If in fact the owner goes to prison, unless someone comes forward to run it. And I'm not sure just who that might be."

"You are right," Maria Crawford agrees. "The wife could hardly run it by herself."

"Unless perhaps Mike and Alexis Sobranos, his friend in London at the travel agency, decide to take it over. That might be a solution," Sam speculates, making patterns on the tablecloth with a spoon.

"Brilliant, Old Man," Charlie speaks, "I never gave that a thought. That Alexis could make a go of it if anyone could. And with Mike's connections at the travel agency, why they'd be set up pretty. Bookings galore."

"Bookings wouldn't be a problem," Emma agrees, "But what about the mother? Sorry to puncture the bubble, but she wouldn't want to be displaced, would she?"

"Possibly not," Sam agrees, "but if your alternative is closing down completely and you have a family to feed, well, that makes a difference." He rubs his chin thoughtfully. "Besides, she may just be ready to chuck the responsibility and ease into semi-retirement."

"Then too," Jane adds, "she owes a debt to Alexis's family. They took Lydia in when things were awfully unpleasant at home."

They continue to speculate until the Neptune gives every appearance of closing. Lights dim, there is a hurried bustle of staff toward the kitchens carrying the odd glass, the crumpled napkin. The head waiter magically appears at the door to usher out their party and a few other lingering guests.

The evening has taken wings, Emma realizes, and their Greek idyll is coming quickly to an end. What has it all meant, Emma considers as the party begins breaking up. A better understanding of the Greeks and their fierce love of country, a new appreciation of the humble shepherd in the Bassae hills who seems now a real person in her memory, and finally, a sincere appreciation of her English friends and their contributions to the return of the amulet to its rightful place.

Whatever happens next, Emma thinks as they make their goodbyes to Plato, the amulet is safe. George Soutakis, wherever you are, I hope you are at peace.

TWELVE

Mozart's Magic Flute at Glyndebourne

Leaving England is more painful than a troublesome toothache that won't go away Emma muses in her room, as she sits, surrounded by piles of clothing she is unable to fit into her case.

In the brief time since her return from Athens she has been interviewed by William Clark at the Celia Drummond school. She finds him a friendly, outgoing man of about sixty, dapper in a Savile Row suit and a silk tie of the most resonant reseda she has ever seen.

He is of a type, Emma thinks, a well-dressed Englishmen with well-groomed silver hair, typical of many walking the streets of London every day. The sort of person, not an expert on art by any means, but knowledgeable, and successful in his job as director of the school.

He promptly offers her the post of art lecturer, promising to give her a free hand in planning the gallery visits each week. With an art history degree from the University of Virginia and two semesters under Maria Crawford at London University, she might be overqualified, here the brown eyes twinkle mischievously, but that is Celia Drummond's gain, what? Good humor pervades the man's personality. And the amount he proposes to pay Emma seems more than generous.

They agree she will begin the third week in September, when she has returned from two weeks in America. Emma assures him that she looks forward to the lectures and will convey that enthusiasm to her students. Then he asks her if getting around on the Underground will be a problem. She replies confidently that it will not. That it is by far the best and most economical way to traverse London. They will not be needing expensive taxis, she assures him. She says this with a certain amount of pride, spoken like a true Londoner, she thinks, recalling her remarks.

As she continues coping with the packing, she reflects on how difficult saying goodbye to Frances Belfrage and her husband Richard will be. They have served nobly *in loco parentis*, on hand when she needed advice but respecting her age and independence as she wishes. Emma feels an enormous affection for them both.

They understand perfectly when she tells them she will be leaving. She and Jane have decided to share a tiny flat on Russell Square in the autumn. Located in the heart of literary Bloomsbury, it seems the perfect site to them both. Near London University and the British Museum, they will be in an area dotted with literary and artistic associations, notably the Bloomsbury group of artists and writers. She and Jane will move in when she returns from her trip home in mid-September and Jane begins her studies at Birkbeck College. Emma is looking forward to being truly on her own. With Jane's level-headed, calm personality, things are certain to run smoothly.

Sam's decision to accept the post in Aberdeen means they will enjoy the months together before January, when he is scheduled to depart. But Emma chooses to put January firmly out of mind and to enjoy the present. There is Christmas in Virginia with her family to anticipate. And her parents are planning to write to Sam, inviting him to join them there also.

Miss Crawford's glowing letter of recommendation has gone off to the Corcoran Gallery and an interview in Washington D. C. has been set up while she is in Virginia. But that job is still uncertain, as are her plans for the new year.

In her letter Miss Crawford has included a few lines about Emma's role in the recovery of the Apollo Amulet and the ceremonies in Athens which followed. Her assessment of Emma's abilities as a student assures Emma that she will treasure her copy of the letter as long as she lives. She smiles, confident the future will be bright even though at this point she is uncertain of the time and place when she and Sam will be together.

For her final evening in England, Sam has planned a very special treat. Along with Jane and Charlie, they will be going to a performance at Glyndebourne, the summer opera located in the Sussex countryside. They will catch the afternoon train at Victoria Station, picnic on the grounds of

Glyndebourne manor house during the interval, and enjoy Mozart's opera, The Magic Flute.

They will also see new stage settings designed by the well-known British artist David Hockney which all London is talking about. Especially designed for The Magic Flute, the settings were immediately a hit when revealed at Glyndebourne for the first time. What luck to have precious Glyndebourne tickets, Emma thinks, wondering how Charlie and Sam managed it. She is still feeling apprehensive about traipsing about London in full evening dress in mid-afternoon, bound for Victoria Station to catch the Glyndebourne train.

Emma slips the evening gown over her head. Its richly colored skirt of jeweled floral tones topped by a simple, long-sleeved black chiffon blouse looks becoming. There is a faintly regal look about it, she admits, admiring her reflection in the mirror. She ignores the unfinished packing. It can wait until tomorrow. Her plane doesn't leave until late afternoon.

"A fresh, blooming English rose, a girl bound for Glyndebourne." Frances Belfrage exclaims, coming into the room.

Her face is flushed from the heat of the kitchen where she has baked apple tarts to go into the picnic hamper for the al fresco dinner during the interval of the opera. Sam and Charlie are bringing the hamper laden with additional delicacies.

Emma smiles. When Frances speaks, 'girl' comes out 'gel' in her rich, fluty voice.

"How can I be so lucky?" Emma says. "I've been welcomed into the home of the most wonderful couple in England, studied two semesters with Maria Crawford at London University for which I shall be eternally grateful, found a loyal friend in Jane Hale, and for some zany reason I cannot explain, have been chosen as 'special' by Dr. Sam McGregor. Surely my cup runs over."

"Don't forget the exciting moments in the quest for the Apollo Amulet," Frances adds.

"Meeting with Uncle Scopas, Phaedra and Roberto Gubbio weren't exactly pleasant," Emma reflects, "but yes, they were undisputedly exciting moments."

Emma suddenly turns to the tall, grey-haired woman wearing tweeds, a twin set of sweaters and pearls and hugs her tightly. "Oh, Frances, I will miss you and Richard so much."

"But you'll be in London, at least for a while. We'll see you of course," Frances answers smoothly. But she too, knows in her heart it will be different with Emma living in Russell Square. Emma has almost taken the place of the child she and Richard never had.

The street buzzer sounds and Emma hurries to answer.

"Emma, It's Sam. I've got Jane and Charlie here in the taxi. I'll be right up to collect you." Emma presses the buzzer which opens the downstairs door.

This is the first time she has seen Sam in evening dress. How handsome he looks. As they face each other at the door of the Belfrage flat there are a few moments of mutual, unspoken admiration.

Frances hurries from the kitchen bearing a carefully-wrapped package of tarts. Sam and Emma make their goodbyes and she watches them hurry to the lift. Their joy and happiness makes Frances recall a certain Surrey moonlight picnic, when she and Richard were younger.

Downstairs, Sam and Emma sail past Hawkins, who swells with pride as he opens the door for them. Emma feels self-conscious as she hurries to the taxi, being careful to keep her skirts off the pavements. It is mid-afternoon, and they are wearing evening clothes in central London! Whatever will people think?

She needn't have worried. Pedestrians politely ignore them as they climb into the taxi. When they pull into Victoria Station, similarly dressed couples in evening dress are hurrying along, women mindful of their dresses, men staggering under the weight of large picnic hampers as they board the train.

Indeed the Glyndebourne platform at Victoria Station is thronged with opera goers. As the train glides away, some high spirited opera buffs begin popping champagne corks, but Jane eyes them with disapproval.

"Why they won't be in any condition to enjoy the Mozart," Jane observes primly.

Oh Jane, thinks Emma, you are a treasure.

The train speeds toward Sussex, backyard gardens filled with late summer roses and dahlias give way to green countryside, stopping occasionally at commuter stations on the route. Emma loves train journeys. She views them as one giant continuous landscape painting, eternally unfolding, each different sighting fresh and new.

Early fall asters and Michelmas daisies are at their finest, growing wild along the tracks. Some of the little station gardens, lovingly tended, exhibit riotous displays of dahlias, late roses and 'chrysants' as the Sloane Street flower vendor has taught Emma to call chrysanthemums.

Emma recalls the landscape painters England has produced as the train jostles along. By now they are getting close to Sussex, the very place Turner loved to paint. Samuel Palmer, whose unique vision gave birth to the sublime, ephemeral Shoreham landscape paintings he created in Sussex. No wonder England boasts such gifted painters. The whole of the countryside is one giant garden, Emma reflects.

Checking the hamper at the cloakroom, the four wander through the beautiful gardens of Glyndebourne, speculating on just where they might set up their picnic at the interval. Emma and Sam stroll behind Jane and Charlie in the gloaming. Sam unexpectedly veers off the path, leading Emma to a tiny rustic twig bench barely big enough for two, hidden in a bower of blooming honeysuckle. There is a small pond, in which they can just make out large orange carp lazily swimming.

"We mustn't lose Jane and Charlie," Emma says.

"Not to worry. We'll catch them up in a tick," Sam answers, fishing into a pocket and bringing out a small box of a pale blue velvet. Solemnly he presents it to her.

"This is for you, Emma, a wee gift."

She opens the lid and takes out a ring, a large garnet surrounded by a circle of smaller rose-colored stones. "How beautiful!" she exclaims, passing it to him. He slips it on her finger as she peers at it.

"I've never seen such a beautiful setting. What are the smaller stones?"

"Rose diamonds. One never sees them anymore. I can't think why. It was my great-grandmother's engagement ring. It's Victorian, of course. You don't think it's too old fashioned for you?" His voice is anxious.

She shakes her head firmly. "Of course not, I love it."

"Then to Emma, with my love," Sam says, kissing her soundly in the seclusion of the honeysuckle vines.

Emma's heart pounds as he adds, "For all the world to see."

"Oh, Sam, who would have thought our magical summer would end like this? What if we'd stayed in another pensione, instead of the Pensione Anastasia?"

"Who can say?" Sam answers her softly, kissing her hand with the sparkling stones winking up at them. "One thing is sure, we wouldn't have become embroiled in the disappearing amulet, now would we?" He gazes at her fondly.

"Under different circumstances, in another place, you might have set your eyes on Jane, or even Primrose Wise!" Emma's voice is teasing. In the fast fading light his face is impossible to read. Only a delicate skein of moonlight highlights his blond hair.

"Shame on you, Emma! Have I given my finest feelings to a heartless tease? But yes, we owe a lot to the romantic and rustic Pensione Anastasia! We'll have to return someday, with our brood of children and grandchildren!" Sam's voice holds a promise, she is sure of it.

Round and round her finger she twirls the ring as the magnificent harmonies of Mozart reverberate through the auditorium. Somehow this evening has become the encapsulation of all the events of summer. Brought into focus by Mozart, most gifted of all composers, Emma's spirits rise correspondingly with the swelling chords of the music.

In the stage settings of the brilliant David Hockney, the music seems to take on an additional luster. And the ring, what a marvelous surprise Sam has planned for this evening! She keeps glancing at the shimmer of the stones in her lap.

Who will be the first to notice the ring as they make their way to the picnic? Emma wonders, Jane or Charlie? Even in the late light of an English summer, the twilight is lengthening; soon it will be dark.

The two couples reclaim their basket and stroll outside during the interval, candles twinkling around them as picnics get underway. For them, summer is ending, autumn will be following close on its heels. And a new season of adventure may present itself, who can say?

Whatever comes, Emma knows she will always remember the wonderful Grecian adventure which began at the Pensione Anastasia, and ended at Glyndebourne. Sitting under the stars, wearing Sam's ring, on her finger, Emma, with Sam beside her, is content as she drinks in the beauty of the scene before her while she dreams.

Bronze Head of Athena, Over Life size,
By Cephisodorus, intended for a site in Piraeus

ACKNOWLEDGMENTS

Help for the writer can, and does, arrive in many ways: an unexpected afternoon of solitude, a surprise telephone message of encouragement, a glowing letter from a reader when one is struggling, a sepia memory flash of a spectacular incident, long forgotten.

Perhaps, however, the greatest help comes from people.

My grateful thanks to the many friends, near and far, who in so many ways helped me write this book, friends like librarians Candice Michalik of the Lynchburg Public Library and Bonnie Stelzer of the Delray Beach Library, to Helen Morrison, Ruth and Gene Crabb, Daisy Oblinger and the Piedmont Writers Group; Don and Mary Marquandt, Molly Jenkins, Mary Ellett, Gay Tucker, Pat Wilson, Joy Frost, Jackie Moffatt, Sandy Wesley, Delores Cavallo and other Pen Women in Lynchburg and in Boca Raton.

Thanks also to Kathy Fryer, Grace Carey, Harriett Hellewell, Ginny McCraw, Elizabeth Ford, Elizabeth Lipscomb, James Whitehead, Nan Carmack, Barbara Provan and Sylvia Wilcox; to Reed Finlay and the Dante Aligheri Society of Virginia; to George and Anastasia Savramis and Christine and George Peters, my consultants on matters Greek; to my family Daisy Warnalis, Holly Williams and my husband Jim; and to the memory of Professor Maria Shirley, who first showed me the glorious Temple of Apollo at Bassae.

READER'S COMMENTS ON *REMEMBERING PIERO*

"Alice Heard Williams' novel is a fictional account of Maddalena dei Crespi who has to decide between the successful fifteenth century artist Piero della Francesca and the more ardent Luigi Castellani. The novel, like those of John Grisham, is fast-paced with new developments in each chapter. The thorough research into details of the time is impressive."

Reed Finlay writing in *La Gazetta di Dante,* Virginia

~

"I just had a wonderful experience—I read *Remembering Piero.* So lyrical, colorful and emotional. I loved the characters and felt I was transformed back in time. When your book arrived I was plowing through two very long biographies. When I started your book I was immediately engaged and couldn't put it down."

Charlotte Jacobs, Professor of Medicine, Stanford University, California

"Wonderful *Remembering Piero* arrived in yesterday's mail. What marvelous insight into Italian life of an earlier century! I'm sending copies to three friends in Italy. Eagerly awaiting your next book."

Terry Stacy, Kentucky.

~

"I ordered *Remembering Piero,* a beautiful book, and it is delightful reading. I marvel at your style and can well appreciate the amount of research that went into it. Congratulations!"

Ruth Ann Jobin, Colorado.

~

"In *Remembering Piero* Williams goes father back in time than in her novel on Vincent van Gogh, Seeking the High Yellow Note, to life in fifteenth century Italy, including a massive flood and subsequent suffering."

Skip Sheffield, Boca Raton FL News.

~

"In the book Piero della Francesca's art is brilliantly described and the book is well focused and constructed. The difficulty is setting it aside between chapters. The drama unfurls in the midst of civil intrigue and a disaster when the River Arno floods, threatening damage to many priceless works of art."

Joy Frost, reviewing in *The Pen Woman.*

~

"In *Remembering Piero* you made the artist come alive. I am reading your book for the second time and thoroughly enjoying it! Thank you."

Eleanor Jensen, Florida.

"The book follows the artist's life and features characters from the de Medici family. The world of the Renaissance seems real in Alice Heard Williams' book, *Remembering Piero*."

Mike Shands, Watauga County, NC *Mountain Times*.

BVG